Wanda Griess 2012

M000211388

Gently to a kill

Former Treasury Secretary and City tycoon, Sir Charles Stanton, and his second wife, Daphne, have a shared passion – English classical landscape paintings, a notable collection of which is housed in Warren Lodge, Sir Charles's country house, remotely situated in the forest and breckland country of West Suffolk. Living with them are their son Timothy, himself a would-be painter, and their daughter Cassandra, recently married to a forest-conservator Hugh Merton; while staying at the Lodge are the art historian, Leslie Phipps, who is engaged on a book about the Stanton Collection, and photographer Dennys Brewster, who is to supply the illustrations.

Out of the blue there arrives at the Lodge the son of Sir Charles's first marriage, who, for the past twenty years, has been pursuing his career in Australia. Laurence Stanton has made a name for himself as a writer of espionage thrillers, and his delighted father is prepared to go to any lengths to keep him in England. Not surprisingly, 'the Aussie' is less than popular at Warren Lodge, but unpopularity seems an insufficient reason for the fate soon to overtake him. One Sunday afternoon he fails to return from a walk in the forest; his body is found; he has been shot with a shot-gun; and the gun is traceable to the gun-room at the Lodge.

Strings are pulled by a distraught Sir Charles, and Chief Superintendent George Gently is dispatched to unravel the tragedy, his brief being to keep the affair in the lowest possible profile; but as he begins to piece it together an unexpected element comes into the reckoning, and events mount uncontrollably to a harrowing conclusion on the lonely brecks.

Other murder cases investigated
by Chief Superintendent Gently, CID.

GENTLY TO A KILL

Alan Hunter

Constable · London

First published in Great Britain 1992
by Constable & Company Limited
3 The Lanchesters, 162 Fulham Palace Road, London W6 9ER
Copyright © 1992 by Alan Hunter
The right of Alan Hunter to be
identified as the author of this work
has been asserted by him in accordance
with the Copyright, Designs and Patents Act 1988
ISBN 0 09 470830 4
Set in Linotron 11pt Palatino
and printed in Great Britain by
Redwood Press Limited
Melksham, Wiltshire

A CIP catalogue record for this book
is available from the British Library

The characters and events in this book are
fictitious; the locale is sketched from life.

For Judy Saxton
Romance-writer Extraordinary

1

For some reason – it was probably symptomatic – the modest station lacked a sign-board. Leaning out of the train window, Gently called:

'Would this be Breckford Station?'

Two coaches away, a porter with rolled shirt-sleeves was loading mailbags on to a trolley. He straightened up to stare at Gently before answering:

'Ah. This here is Breckford.'

Apart from the porter, the platform was deserted. All that neighboured it was a wood-yard. Then there was a screen of oaks and beeches, and beyond, encircling them, the gloom of many pines. A roof showed distantly among the trees. A rough country of bracken, gorse and solitary fir-trees hemmed the pines. Then there was a slow-flowing reedy river, drawing a line beneath these. But of the town, if there was one, appeared no sign.

Gently got down, lugging his bag. It was mid-June, and the sun struck hot.

Across in the wood-yard a saw was shrieking, and the sad smell of raped pine hung in the air.

Slowly, reluctantly, the train drew out, and now one could see a cluster of houses, a stone bridge with several arches, a malthouse, a squat church tower. The porter came by, shoving his trolley. Gently fell into step beside him.

'Which way to the police station?'

'Keep a-goin', old partner. You can't miss it.'

'It's in the main street?'

'Blast, yes. We've only got one street in Breckford.'

But across the line he paused to stare again at Gently, at his bag, his city clothes. He jerked a thumb over his shoulder.

'You've come about that job up there, squire?'

Just then, a police Escort swung into the station yard, and an anxious-looking moustached man got out and hastened towards them.

'Sir – Chief Superintendent Gently? They've only just rung us to expect you . . .!'

He grabbed Gently's bag. Across in the wood-yard, the saw had begun to shriek afresh. They left the porter gazing after them and sapiently nodding his head. The moustached man opened the car door for Gently, and seemed even inclined to help belt him in.

'You stay, Gently.'

It was earlier that morning when the conference at the Yard was just breaking up. Colleagues, clutching files, were pushing past him through the door of the Assistant Commissioner (Crime)'s office. Nothing sensational had come in overnight, and Gently's own file was light – a couple of reports to write up, and neither of them strictly urgent. The office door closed; the AC beckoned him to the desk.

'Now. I've been talking to Tommy. What do you know about Sir Charles Stanton?'

'Sir Charles . . . you mean, the politician?'

'Yes, Gently – the politician! He was Secretary to the Treasury a few years back, and resigned to take a post in the City. Last year he retired with a golden handshake, and now lives in Suffolk and collects paintings. You wouldn't have run across him, would you?'

Gently shook his head.

'Well, he's heard of you, probably from Tommy.' 'Tommy' was Sir Thomas Bedingfield KCB, the Suffolk Chief Constable. The AC frowned. 'There's been a tragedy up there. A shooting. Stanton's eldest son. On Sunday he went for a walk in the forest and failed to return to the house. They found the body yesterday. He'd been shot in the back with a shot-gun. The shot-gun belonged to a brother-in-law, a Hugh Merton, and it's him the locals fancy. But it seems the family don't like the idea, which is why they've come screaming to us.'

'Screaming for me?'

'Who else? Since that Eastgate job you're Tommy's blue-eyed boy. He wants you to use your famous discretion and wind the whole thing up at the coroner's inquest.'

Gently didn't look thrilled. 'Would that be possible?'

'That, Gently, is what you are going to find out.'

'Have they much on Merton?'

'Nothing final. But a paraffin test they did was positive.'

The AC flicked open a file that lay before him and ran a frowning eye over the contents. He turned a sheet.

'According to Merton, he was shooting rabbits on the Saturday. That would account for the positive test. But then there's propinquity and motive.'

'Propinquity . . .?'

'Oh yes. Merton is something to do with the Forestry. On Sunday afternoon he was out there, he admits, checking a newly replanted section. That wasn't where the body was found, but it wasn't so far away.'

'And . . . motive?'

'Ah – motive. Very briefly, I'll put you in the picture. The deceased was the son of Stanton's first marriage, and had only recently returned from Australia. Stanton hadn't seen him for twenty years. He wanted him to stay. He offered him a cottage due to fall vacant on the estate, but which he'd offered previously to the Mertons.'

'And that's it?'

9

'It could have been enough, Gently. Men have been shot in the back for less. And don't forget the gun. Out of eight in the gun-room, Merton's was the only one recently fired.' The AC turned a sheet. 'He claims he cleaned it on the Saturday before he put it back on the rack. Perhaps he would have cleaned it on Sunday too, but didn't get the chance.'

'Eight guns . . .'

'It's a country estate, where you would expect to find guns. Warren Lodge, near Breckford. That's shooting country if I know anything.'

'But . . . my job is to get Merton off?'

'Tcha!' The AC clicked his tongue. 'If he's guilty, of course you'll nail him, or anyone else with their neck stuck out. But discretion's the word. It could just have been an accident, with all those guns lying around. Merton could have shot the fellow by chance, and now be too scared to admit it. Something like that. So keep it low key, unless you find a case that we can't close our eyes to. Latchford Police are handling the job, but you'll report to them at Breckford. Understood?'

'Understood.'

The AC closed the file and handed it to Gently.

'I almost envy you,' he said. 'A little job in the country in this weather. Give Suffolk my love.'

Gabrielle, when he rang her from his office, expressed almost the same sentiments.

And then, because his car was in dock, he'd gone to do battle with Liverpool Street Station.

'Detective Chief Inspector Calthorpe, sir, of Latchford CID. I don't know if you've had lunch, sir, but The Cross Keys is as good as anywhere.'

They'd cleared the station yard and were ascending the modest, crooked street, where the two-storey shops and

10

houses were almost all built in flint. Somehow it gave Breckford a miserable air, a general aspect of greyness. One felt one had strayed over a boundary into some half-forgotten tribal territory.

'I had a bite on the train. That'll hold me for now. Where's Merton?'

'At the police station, sir. I thought you'd like to see him first thing.'

'Before that, I'd like a complete run-down! All those things that aren't in the report.'

'Well . . . yes, sir.'

Calthorpe looked serious. Besides the moustache he wore a black bow-tie. He drove the Escort with careful attention, didn't take his eyes off the road when he spoke.

They turned right to park at the police station, a Victorian structure in dismal red brick. Inside it smelled of soot, and indeed there was a fireplace in reception.

'DS Bodney, sir . . . and DC Thompson.'

Gently shook hands with Calthorpe's understrappers; the one a ham-faced man with untidy fair hair, the other a hefty youngster wearing a bomber-jacket.

'If we could have some coffee . . .'

Calthorpe led the way to a cramped office with too few chairs; Gently sat, Calthorpe sat; the Sergeant and DC remained standing. Gently unzipped his bag and laid the file on the desk. He filled his pipe and lit it, blew smoke into the sooty air.

'Now! Let's have some background. Was that Warren Lodge I could see across the river?'

'It . . . Yes, sir! Warren Lodge. Sir Charles and Lady Daphne Stanton.'

'A shooting estate?'

'I believe so, sir. It's mostly breckland and forest. The Forestry lease a good part of it, but the brecks go on for miles.'

'So who owns those guns?'

'That's just the point, sir!' Calthorpe said eagerly. 'The rest belong to Sir Charles and Lady Daphne, there's just this spare one belonging to Merton. It's his, and he admits it. And that was the gun that had been fired. And it had been wiped off before it was racked. And Merton has a key to the gun-room.'

'The gun had been wiped? You're sure?'

'Well, there weren't any dabs on it, sir.'

Calthorpe signalled to Bodney, who unlocked a steel cabinet and produced from it a double-barrelled twelve-bore shot-gun. Calthorpe handed it to Gently.

'You take a look, sir.'

Gently broke the gun and took a look. One barrel was bright and oily, the other dimmed and streaked with soot.

'How does Merton explain that?'

'He can't, sir. Swears he hasn't used the gun since Saturday. Afterwards he ran a pull-through through both barrels, and then he did wipe it before he hung it up.'

'So . . . if he missed cleaning one of the barrels?'

Calthorpe looked startled. 'Not likely, sir. Too much of a coincidence for him to do that, just the day before his brother-in-law was shot.'

Gently closed the gun softly and laid it on the desk by the file. 'Now the set-up,' he said. 'Who else lives at the Lodge. And where they all were on Sunday afternoon.'

'Yes, sir.' Calthorpe seemed to brace himself. 'Well, there's Sir Charles and Lady Daphne. Then there's their daughter, who's married to Merton, and another son, Timothy Stanton. Then there's the two people they have staying with them, Mr Phipps and Mr Brewster. And a cook–housekeeper and a maid . . . Myhill and Brett, I think their names are. There's an outside man and a daily help, but they're only there on weekdays.'

'And who are these guests?'

'They're not actually guests, sir. They're both there doing

a job. Mr Phipps is writing a book about Sir Charles's pictures, and Mr Brewster is taking the photographs for it.'

Gently puffed. 'So you've taken their statements.'

'Yes, sir . . . they're in the drawer . . .'

'Just a résumé!'

'Of course, sir!' Calthorpe jerked himself a little straighter. 'Lady Daphne and her daughter, sir, went riding after lunch. They keep two horses in the stables there. And it was them who heard the shot.'

'Where were they then?'

'Away on the brecks, sir. But they heard this shot back in the forest. Put it down to someone having a bang at the rabbits. They give the time as about three thirty.'

'And Merton, where was he at three thirty?'

'He was around, sir, he has to admit it. Claims he was inspecting a replanted section of the forest, which would put him half a mile away from where we found the body. He's got some excuse about why he was there . . . he's an Assistant Conservator or something.'

'A Forestry Officer.'

'Right, sir. He's been living at the Lodge since he married the daughter. And they'd set their hearts on having that cottage, which is right handy for his job at the Forestry Centre.'

'Ye-es,' Gently said. 'Where was Sir Charles?'

'In the TV lounge, sir, all the afternoon. He was watching the World Cup matches, and Mr Brewster, the photographer, was with him for most of the time. Before that, he was in the library. And Mr Phipps was down the garden. It was a bit of luck, him being down there, because it was him who saw Laurence Stanton, that's the deceased, on his way to the forest, and likewise he heard the row that led up to it.'

'A – row?'

'I was coming to it, sir! There was a bit of ill-feeling between the stepbrothers. According to Mr Phipps, and we've only his word for it, it was over Sir Charles's

13

secretary.' Calthorpe looked a little pink. 'A Miss Emma Spinks, sir. I didn't quite get round to her just now. But it seems like Timothy Stanton fancies her, and his step-brother was getting in his light.'

'And this Miss Spinks resides at the Lodge?'

'Yes, sir. Sorry, sir. I've got her statement. She was walking Sir Charles's two retrievers, but that was on the brecks, going the other way.'

Gently stared, ran his fingers over the gun. 'So now we come to Timothy Stanton.'

'Yes, sir.' Calthorpe took a swallow. 'After lunch, he went back to his houseboat.'

'His what?'

'His houseboat, sir. That's where he lives, on a house-boat. The river borders the grounds and there's a private mooring close to the house. He's a bit of a painter or something, and anyway, he lives on this houseboat. So after lunch he went back there, and it seems his stepbrother went there too, and Mr Phipps heard them rowing down there, though he wasn't where he could see them. Then the next thing he sees Laurence Stanton stalking off towards the forest, and as far as we know that was the last time Laurence Stanton was seen alive.'

'And . . . Timothy Stanton?'

'Stayed on the houseboat. Till he came back up for his tea.'

'While our Mr Phipps remained in the garden?'

'Yes, sir, that's what he says. There's a garden settee down there, and he took the Sunday papers with him.'

Gently went on fingering the gun. 'Would Timothy Stanton have passed him, going back to the house?'

Calthorpe was silent a moment. 'No, sir. He didn't have to go through the garden.'

'And might Timothy Stanton have a key to the gun-room?'

14

Calthorpe was silent even longer. 'You wouldn't be suggesting, sir . . .?'

Gently blew smoke-rings. 'Why not? He seems to have had equal opportunity, and a classic when it comes to motive.'

'But . . . his own stepbrother, sir!'

'Stepchildren aren't notably affectionate with each other.'

'But – that's Merton's gun! And we know that *he* was in the forest.'

'On his own admission.' Gently blew another ring. 'But of course it needn't rest there. We have our two lady horse-riders, hearing a shot a long way off. Then there is well-fancied Miss Spinks with only retrievers for an alibi, and, of course, our Mr Phipps, who at least knew where to look for the victim. And in the end, might it not have been an accident, say someone stumbling with a gun? Surely that has happened before, within the ken of Latchford Police?'

Calthorpe's grave eyes had rounded, and Bodney and Thompson were gaping. For a brief interval there was silence in the office, broken only by a stir of traffic in the street. Then Calthorpe pulled himself together.

'No, sir – no! And do you know why? It's because we've had the PM report since we sent you that file. It wasn't the shot that finished Stanton. It was his bleeding to death afterwards. Someone shot him and left him to die – and that makes it murder in my book.'

Gently stared at him. 'Show me that report.'

Calthorpe jerked open a drawer and produced the document.

Laurence Stanton had received injuries to lung and spine, but emphatically the cause of death was blood-loss. Cause of injuries: a spread of shot, fired from an approximate distance of twelve feet.

'Let me see the photographs.'

Calthorpe handed them to him. They showed Stanton

lying face-down. Extended: his right arm, as though he'd been trying to drag himself along. The shirt was ragged and blood-soaked; blood had spread on the ground beside him. A long shot showed bracken, gorses, but only a handful of small birch trees.

'And this is in the forest?'

'Yes, sir. Right on the edge, where it joins the brecks. The ride ends there in a little dell. It's about a mile from the house.'

'Is there any cover?'

'It's all cover, sir. There's brambles and bushes and all sorts. We reckon chummie crept up on him behind an old holly bush. It's about the distance it says down here.'

'It needn't have been an ambush.'

'Sir?'

'The killer may have approached Stanton openly. Then fired the shot as he walked away. It might well have been an accidental discharge.'

Calthorpe shook his head firmly. 'No, sir. Never. That gun was pointed when it went off. It might be as you say, but it wasn't an accident. Not when chummie left him there to die.'

Gently sucked on a dead pipe. 'And Merton was the man on the spot!'

'Well, he was, sir,' Calthorpe said. 'And we can't forget it was his gun.'

'Weapon, motive and opportunity.'

'That's it, sir. It all adds up.'

Gently sighed, and put down his pipe. 'In that case, let's have him in!'

Calthorpe dismissed Bodney and Thompson, after dispatching the latter for an extra chair. But then coffee was brought in, to be drunk before business recommenced. About Calthorpe now was an air of complacency, of a man

16

who'd made his point; he didn't hurry over his coffee, and even lit himself a sly cheroot. Finally he stubbed it.

'If you're ready, sir . . .?'

Merton was ushered in by Thompson. A tall man, in his mid-thirties, with a freckled, small-featured face and ginger hair. He was wearing a tweed jacket with leathered elbows, an open-necked shirt and corduroys, giving the impression of an outdoor type who'd be quite at home in the brecks and the forest.

He came in sullenly. His eyes went to the gun.

'Sit down, Merton,' Gently said.

As though it were a favour, Merton sat, listened while Gently introduced himself.

'Now, Merton. You know why you are here?'

Merton's eyes were hostile. He said nothing.

'Is there anything you wish to tell us?'

Merton stared back. 'Not a damned thing.'

Gently said: 'You must understand, Merton, that we have grounds for grave suspicion. If there is some explanation for what happened on Sunday, you would be well advised to give it now.'

'Go to hell.'

'It would be in your interest. As it stands, you are in danger of a serious charge.'

'I said go to hell!'

Slowly, Gently nodded. 'Very well. Then we'll just go over your statement again.'

Merton glared at him. He had angry blue eyes and a determined, thrust-out jaw. His eyes switched bitterly to the gun, then back again to Gently.

'Any reason why I should?'

Gently shrugged. 'Any reason why you shouldn't?'

'Yes, there is! Because all you're after is to shove me in a bit deeper. There isn't a case. The yokels know it. That's why you have been brought down here. I know Sir Charles, he won't rest till someone has paid for his beloved

17

first-born. And it isn't going to be me, you hear? There isn't a case, and you know it.'

'You were not responsible.'

'I – no!'

'Then isn't it in your interest to help us?'

'But that's not what you're after!'

'Yet – if you are innocent?'

Merton stared, breathing harder.

Gently said: 'All I am asking is an account of your movements on Sunday. You say you are innocent. I'm ready to accept that. But it still may help to go through them again.'

'To help you. Not me.'

'It could even help you.'

'That's likely.'

'Still . . . shall we say from after lunch on Sunday?'

Merton's stare fell to the gun: a struggle seemed to be going on inside him. He glanced at Calthorpe, who was watching him keenly, then at Gently, then again at the gun.

'All right, then! I suppose I'm a fool, but there's nothing you can hang me for. After lunch, like I said, I went to the stables, to help Cassandra and her mother saddle up.'

'This would be when?'

'Two, or soon after. It was probably half-past when I saw them away. And no, I didn't go back to the gun-room for my gun – it was Sunday, remember? We don't shoot on Sundays.'

'The gun-room being where?'

Merton's mouth twisted. 'Next to the stables. Didn't they tell you? Oh yes! I could have slipped that gun out, without a soul around to see me.'

'But . . . you didn't.'

'No, I didn't. I had other things on my mind. Robinson, one of the rangers, had reported pine-tip moth in section 10. Do I have to explain?'

'If you will.'

'Well, it's a pest that attacks the pine seedlings. The

18

caterpillars feed on the tips of the seedlings and cause malformations when the trees grow up. It's a serious matter, and it's part of my job to assess what action needs to be taken. And section 10 was where I went on Sunday. There, and nowhere else at all.'

'You went there directly?'

'Yes . . . no! If you want me to be so bloody precise. First, I went back into the house to fetch my jacket and change into boots.'

Gently paused. 'Did you meet anyone there?'

'No. Should I have done?'

'Did you meet, or see anyone at all, either in the house or in the grounds, later?'

Merton's eyes had gone still. 'This is one of your tricky ones, isn't it?' he said. 'You think perhaps I saw a certain person on his way towards the forest. Well, forget it. I didn't see him. I didn't see anyone at all. Not in the house. Not in the grounds. And please don't take me for a bloody fool.'

'You didn't see Laurence Stanton.'

'No.'

'Then . . . or later.'

Merton turned his eyes up.

'Nor, for example, your brother-in-law Timothy?'

Merton hesitated. Then shook his head.

'So,' Gently said. 'You left for the forest. Would the time perhaps have been around a quarter to three?'

'If you say so. I didn't check. It could have been earlier or later than that.'

'And you took the shortest route to this section 10.'

'Yes, I did. The direct route. You follow the main ride for quarter of a mile, then take a cross-ride towards 10.'

'The main ride being the one that Laurence Stanton would have followed?'

Merton snapped: 'Just go to hell!'

Gently glanced at Calthorpe. 'Yes, sir,' Calthorpe

19

responded promptly. 'There's a field-gate into it from the Lodge grounds, and it goes straight through the forest to the place where we found him. Then there's a cross-ride from there over to section 10. I'd say that was as direct a way as any.'

'It's a bloody half-mile further!' Merton exclaimed. 'And I'm tramping the rides enough as it is. I was on Forestry business, remember? Not going for a stroll to take the air.'

'I wouldn't say half a mile,' Calthorpe said.

'Bloody half a mile or more!'

'I'd say about the same distance, sir,' Calthorpe said.

Merton glared at him, breathed faster.

Gently said: 'Did you take the main ride, Merton?'

'For the last time – no, I didn't! I took the cross-ride, the way I said, and then past section 9 to 10.'

'And saw no one at any time.'

'Do I have to repeat that again?'

Gently stroked the gun. 'So you arrived at section 10. Would you put the time at about three p.m.?'

'I suppose so.'

'And you were there for how long?'

'I don't know! Say as long as it took.'

'Perhaps an hour?'

'Yes, it may have been.'

'So you were there at half-past three.'

'Yes. There. In section 10.'

'When, according to witness, the shot was fired.'

Merton simply glared at him. But his face was paler.

Gently said: 'Wouldn't you have heard the shot?'

'Bloody no. Why should I have heard it?'

'How far away were you?'

'Too damn far! And there were trees in the way, weren't there?'

Calthorpe said: 'It's about half a mile, sir. But there's this cross-ride linking with 10. And it was still enough on Sunday. I'd say it was possible to have heard the gun.'

'Perhaps we could experiment,' Gently said.

'Listen, listen!' Merton gabbled. 'So I may have heard it. But it didn't register. I was there doing my job, remember, and there's lots of shooting goes on around here.'

'But – on a Sunday?'

'I tell you it didn't register.'

'Not even later, when you'd heard what had happened?'

'Not even then. Simply it didn't. I was doing my job, and I didn't notice.'

Gently shrugged, went on stroking. Merton stared at him with anguished eyes. He was certainly paler. And now there was a shine of moisture on his freckled brow.

'Right, then! You finished what you were doing. By which route did you return to the Lodge?'

'By the same one. The shortest. I didn't have any reason to do otherwise.'

'And you arrived at the Lodge when?'

'I don't know! Soon after four. And no, I didn't sneak round to the yard and slip any guns back on the rack! I went straight in, by the front door, and went to change and freshen up before tea. Then I joined the others in the lounge. You only have to ask them.'

'Yet this gun had been taken and used.'

'So it had. But not by me.'

'And that is all you can tell us?'

Merton stuck his chin out and glared at Gently.

'Very well – for now.' Gently nodded to Calthorpe, who rose and touched Merton on the shoulder. Merton gaped.

'You're not – you're not keeping me here?'

'I must ask you to remain here for the moment, Mr Merton.'

'But this is ridiculous! I want a lawyer!'

'You are, of course, entitled to a telephone call.'

'But – but – !'

He seemed unable to believe it. He almost reeled out of

21

the office. Calthorpe returned wearing the ghost of a smirk, but repressed it before he faced Gently.

'So what do you think, sir?'

Gently shook his head. 'We shall probably need a witness to sort out Merton. He isn't the type to confess, and all we have so far is circumstantial.'

'I'll put some men on it, sir . . . but what do you think?'

Gently found the local man a grin. 'First, I think we'd better talk to the others! But before that I want to go over the ground.'

'Yes, sir . . . but you'll have an idea?'

'Put this gun away, and let's go.'

Calthorpe put the gun away, spoke to Bodney, then ushered Gently to the waiting Escort. Outside, the grey, flint-faced town seemed half asleep in the afternoon sun. Its crooked street sagged down to the river, ending there at the ungainly bridge; beyond, the rough country of the brecks and the dark reef of the spreading pine forest. Few vehicles were passing, few pedestrians occupied the pavements. Distantly, one heard the shriek of the saw in the wood-yard. Then there were those roofs above the far-off trees.

2

But as they approached the Escort the door of a car across the street was flung open, and a woman jumped out, slamming the door behind her with vigour. She strode across to them, ignoring a van, which had to brake squeakily to avoid her, and planted herself firmly between them and the Escort.

'Oh dear . . . it's his missus, sir!'

Mrs Merton fixed determined eyes on Gently. A sturdy, somewhat full-faced young woman with chestnut hair and a pouted mouth, she was dressed in a green sweater and tailored tweed skirt.

'I've come for Hugh – where is he?'

'Mrs Merton?' Gently said.

'Yes, Mrs Merton! And you, I take it, are the man Daddy has brought down from London – what's your name? Gently? Well, you're supposed to sort this business out. That's the idea, isn't it? So now, where is Hugh?'

Gently shook his head. 'I'm sorry, Mrs Merton . . .'

'You are the man Daddy sent for, aren't you?'

'I am an officer from the Central Office, seconded to assist the Latchford Police.'

'Yes, that's right. The man Daddy sent for. Well, now I assume you've done your sorting. So just be good enough to produce Hugh, who, among other things, has missed his lunch.'

'I'm afraid it isn't quite so simple, Mrs Merton.'

23

'What?'

'We require your husband just a little longer.'

'Require him? What for?'

'He is assisting us.'

'But, my dear man, he's been here for three hours!' Mrs Merton drew herself up yet further. 'And he didn't even hear the shot, you know, it was Mummy and me who heard that. You must be through with him by now. How can he possibly be assisting you?'

'He is a vital witness.'

'No, he isn't! Good grief, what have the yokels been feeding you? Hugh was half the forest away when Laurence had his accident.'

'His accident . . .?'

'What else? I can tell you, Laurie wasn't used to guns. But the poor fool took one when he went for his stroll, and somehow managed to shoot himself with it. Isn't that so obvious? At least, it is to us. He was probably trailing it and caught it in a bramble. And the sooner you set the yokels right on that, the sooner we can get back to something like normality.'

Gently gazed at her. 'I regret . . .'

'Look, old thing, Hugh must be starving!'

'I cannot yet release your husband.'

'What?'

'He must remain here while we pursue our enquiries.'

Mrs Merton looked as though she might strike him. 'Good God – and you're the man Daddy sent for? Just wait till he hears about this! You'll be back in town before you can spit.'

'And now, if you don't mind, Mrs Merton . . .'

'You really mean this? It isn't just a joke?'

' . . . I have matters to attend to.'

'Great gallons of grief!' For a moment she savaged him with blazing eyes. Then she turned, ran across the street, threw herself in her car and sent it squealing away. A red Peugeot 205 GTi, its registration read CAS 1.

Calthorpe was smirking. 'She's a handful, sir! I had a bit of a go in with her myself.'

Gently made a face. 'Are the rest like her?'

'Her mother's the same breed, sir. The old man is all right.'

'What about the son?'

'He's a bit of a puzzle, sir. But you can get an earful from him, too. Then there's the writer fellow, he's sharp. But the photographer you can get on with.'

'And – the secretary?'

'Well, there you are, sir! She's a tidy slip of a girl.'

They got in the Escort. Calthorpe drove smoothly down the street and over the bridge. At once the small town was left behind, and they were in country, approaching the trees.

'Those are the gates to the Lodge . . .'

They were driving under massive oaks and beeches. To the right, a gravelled drive swung away through stone-pillared gates crowned with carved gryphons. The house itself was hidden by the trees, but probably wasn't very far away. On the left the trees were a thin line through which one could see the rough brecks.

Then, ahead, the pines closed in, threatening the simple country byway, an endless stockade of pink shafts and glooming, impenetrable foliage.

A lane, or ride, departed to the right, separating the forest from the grounds of the house, which here were fenced with rhododendrons, currently lit with purple bloom. Calthorpe turned into this ride. Still the house was concealed from view. But shortly they came to a handsome field-gate, beyond which a drive departed through a succession of shrubberies.

25

'This is the way he would have come?'

'Yes, sir. Through this gate. And that's the main ride through the forest facing it. This one goes on till it comes to the brecks.'

'The ladies, too, came this way?'

'Right, sir. This was their way out there. And Merton.'

'What about the secretary?'

'She'd have gone through the gardens. She took the dogs for a walk by the river.'

Calthorpe parked and they got out. At once one was aware of a resinous perfume. Also of the silence of the ranked trees, which here were sections of Corsican Pine and Scots Fir. Beneath them grew a dense undergrowth of bramble, bracken and snowberry, while stunted elders had taken root on the floor of the ride. There were no birds; but butterflies fluttered about the brambles at the edge of the trees, or sat basking in such patches of sunlight as penetrated the dense canopy.

'Let's go.'

They strode out along the beckoning aisle of the ride. Though straight, it was far from level, and the undergrowth offered plentiful concealment. Clearly there was cover for a stalker who was content to keep his distance; for Merton, if it was he. And Merton was experienced in the ways of the forest. Within a few hundred yards occurred a turn to the right, and at the bend a cross-ride departed.

'Merton's route?'

'So he says, sir. But it doesn't lead direct to section 10.'

Also, the cross-ride was impeded by undergrowth, and appeared an unlikely alternative at any time.

'Have you taken a look at it?'

'Yes, sir. And I couldn't find any trace of it having been used. So I'd say he was lying about that, sir. Whichever way he went, it wasn't up there.'

They continued. At well-spaced intervals two further cross-rides occurred, while the ground cover, if anything,

26

grew more obstructive as they advanced. Creepers of honeysuckle and traveller's joy climbed over the brambles and struggling elders. Bracken and snowberry grew tall, and encroached from the ranks of trees. The ground itself was hard and carpeted with sorrels and dry grass: it retained no footprints, though a faint track showed that occasionally people went that way.

Finally, the gloom ahead was broken, and one saw the silver boles of birches; then, beyond them, a glimpse of the brecks, rising steeply in full sun. The pines ended. They had come to a dell of birches on the very edge of the brecks, separated from them by a wire-netting fence, presumably to exclude rabbits. For the latter were numerous: white tails by the dozen bobbed out of sight as the two men advanced. Then there was a raptor, almost certainly a buzzard, slowly slanting away in the pallid sky.

'Here, sir.'

Not far from the fence the short grass was blackened with congealed stains, while round about were signs of the trampling of many feet. The stains confirmed what the photographs had shown: that Laurence Stanton had fallen forward, head towards the fence. A yard or two back stood the bush that Calthorpe had mentioned. A well-developed holly, it provided cover in plenty.

'We reckon he'd have come out here for a think, sir,' Calthorpe said. 'What with that row with his stepbrother and all. So then he's standing here, looking at the view. And chummie creeps up to this bush and lets fly.'

Yes, it was credible; and more than that, likely. The assassin had cover all the way. Set Stanton where he fell, with his back to the holly, and Calthorpe's scenario was well-nigh irresistible. Gently, too, stood to look at the view, the rise and fall of the ranging brecks, the bracken, the gorse, the rashes of pale grasses, the solitary birches and solitary, gnarled pines.

'What's that over there . . .?'

'An old tank, sir. The army were here during the war.'

Rusty and gun-less, it stood perched on a rise. Perhaps Stanton had been staring at it when he was shot.

Gently went to the fence and hitched himself over. Along the line of the forest ran another faint track. And there was something else. The droppings of a horse. And in a mole-hill, the imprint of a horse's hoof.

Gently beckoned to Calthorpe. 'Were these here yesterday?'

Calthorpe looked sheepish. 'Can't say I noticed, sir!'

'Which way did the ladies say they went?'

'Just out on the brecks, sir. I didn't especially ask where.'

Dung-beetles were busy with the droppings, which clearly had not been deposited lately; and the hoof-mark, also, was blurred: at a guess, could they have been there for forty-eight hours?

The bush had no message, and the ground about had been trampled by policemen and the ambulance-men. Stray shot may have clipped a twig from one of the birches, but that merely completed a too-evident picture.

'Show me the way to this section 10!'

They set off again, along a narrow cross-ride; it began just short of the fatal dell, and dipped down deep through stands of Douglas Firs. The distance was not great, perhaps less than half a mile, and then they emerged at an open plot. Its extent was doubtless a hectare, and at a glance it appeared to contain nothing but weeds; but then one noticed a system of shallow furrows in which were planted young pine seedlings, about a foot in height. Gently bent to examine them, but he wasn't an expert. If the seedlings were infested, he failed to detect it. The ground here, as elsewhere, was rock-hard, and offered no evidence of recent visitings.

'Have you spoken to that forestry worker, Robinson, who Merton claimed put in a report?'

'Well – no, sir! Not yet.' Calthorpe was growing ever more embarrassed.

'Perhaps you'll check on him right away. He could give us a handle for Merton.'

'Yes, sir, as soon as I get back. I'll send Thompson to the Forestry Centre.' Calthorpe hesitated, then: 'But about the sound of the shot, sir . . . don't you think he would have heard it?'

Gently shrugged. 'As I said, we shall probably need an experiment to decide that one.'

They returned by the route claimed by Merton, which may or may not have been shorter, but which ignored two obvious cross-rides to land them in that which was the most obstructed. Dishevelled and perspiring, they regained the car, Calthorpe with a bramble scratch across his cheek.

'What now, sir?'

'Drive me round to the Lodge. Then get on to chasing Robinson.'

Calthorpe was silent on the brief drive that took them through the gates with the two stone gryphons.

'I see you've been in the forest, Gently. In that case, you stand in need of a drink.'

Inevitably, Warren Lodge was a flint-built house, though the flint was dressed, and framed in yellow brick. It occupied rising ground and was nested in trees that included copper beeches. A house built when Victoria was on the throne, with wide sash-windows, discrete wings, and a huge porch.

Before it, a gravel sweep was occupied by quite an assemblage of cars, among which Gently noticed Mrs Merton's red Peugeot GTi. Then stone steps led down to a lawn, neatly contained by clipped yew hedges, and beyond this again shrubberies, and finally another screen of tall trees.

29

'I understand you have met my daughter. I trust I can rely on your charity, Gently. She is obviously gravely upset. Indeed, this is a very saddening business.'

A heavily built man in his mid-sixties, dressed in a suit of thornproof tweed. He had clearly been expecting Gently's visit and had come down the steps as the car pulled up. His full features resembled those of his daughter, and his wiry brown hair was unashamedly dyed; he had brown eyes, full lips and a prominent nose with a trace of a hook. He had thrust out his hand.

'Chief Superintendent Gently?'

'Sir Charles Stanton?'

'Call me Charles. Of course, I've heard about you from Tommy, so you don't come as a complete stranger. Have they put you in the picture? Yes, well. But we can talk about that inside.'

It was the cue for Calthorpe to depart, and he took his cue promptly. Sir Charles led Gently up the steps and into an ornate hall. What one noticed, besides a handsome staircase, were walls almost wholly covered with landscape paintings, some large, some small, and some that could only be regarded as miniatures. Sir Charles waved a dismissive hand towards them.

'I'm afraid this sort of thing gets out of hand! But Daphne is just as crazy as I am. And Timothy wields a brush himself. Do you have pictures?'

'A few.'

'Landscapes?'

'Well . . . a Prout. And a Monet forgery of Detling's.'

'A Detling forgery – yes. It's lucky that fellow stuck to the Impressionists! I suppose you don't want to sell it?'

Gently shook his head.

'Well, I shouldn't know where to hang it, anyway.'

He pushed open a door briskly and ushered Gently into a large lounge. At the far end a lady rose from a sofa, and advanced to meet them. Sir Charles urged Gently forward.

'My dear, our man from the Yard! Gently, meet my wife, Daphne.'

Daphne Stanton offered him a tight little handshake and a stare from a pair of determined grey eyes. She was perhaps ten years younger than her husband, but her blond hair was equally in debt to a bottle. She had lean features and a lean figure and wore a tailored two-piece with a ruffled blouse. In a sharp, contralto voice she said:

'My husband is impossible! Isn't your given name George?'

Gently nodded.

'Then George it is. Even though you're here on this ghastly business.'

Sir Charles, meanwhile, was busy at a cabinet, from which he returned with glasses on a tray: for Gently, a beer; for himself, a scotch; for his wife a stem-glass containing a green liquid.

'Shall we sit down?'

They took their glasses. Lady Daphne resumed her seat on the sofa. She beckoned Gently to a chair next to her. Her husband drew one up to face Gently.

'Cheers.'

They drank.

'Now – getting down to it! I understand you've had a session with my son-in-law. Also, you've been out in the forest. Dare I ask if you have formed an opinion?'

Gently shook his head. 'Not yet.'

Sir Charles stared long; he sipped his drink. 'You know, I feel I'm partly to blame for all this,' he said. 'It bowled me over, seeing Laurence again. I wanted to keep him here at any cost.'

'He intended returning to Australia?'

Sir Charles nodded. 'He had lived there for almost twenty years. He was originally in insurance. His firm sent him out there. He married an Aussie and settled down there. Then he made his name as a writer – espionage

31

thrillers, would you believe? – and dropped insurance. And then his wife left him. And a fortnight ago he walked in here.'

'And . . . you sought to persuade him to stay?'

'Yes. And I think I may have done it.'

'Oh nonsense, Charles!' Lady Daphne said. 'He was like a fish out of water all the time.' She turned eagerly to Gently. 'He'd gone native. He was an Aussie from top to toe. He talked like an Aussie, looked like an Aussie. He might have walked straight out of one of their soaps. Charles didn't recognize him when he turned up here. Oh no. He was going back to Oz.'

Sir Charles drank. 'I admit he had changed,' he said. 'He was only twenty-four when I'd last seen him. Now he was forty, a mature man, and of course he had picked up Australian ways. And he'd taken a knock when his wife ran off. That was his reason for coming over. He was at a crossroads. But I'm still convinced that we could have kept him here.'

'Yes – by offering him Cassie's cottage!'

Sir Charles hunched a little over his glass. 'That was never a settled thing, Daphne.'

'Oh yes it was.' She turned again to Gently. 'Cassandra had been promised it for ever. Bracken Brae Cottage. Down by the river, and only a mile from Hugh's office. When she married him it was understood, they were to have it at Michaelmas, when it fell vacant. It was all planned. Then, out of the blue, Charles offers it to Aussie Laurie.'

'You're being unfair, Daphne.'

'Am I? But Cassie is as much your child as he was. So I'm a jealous bitch, but I can't help it. And Laurie had his own place in Sydney anyway.'

'I admit it was unwise – '

'Unwise. You hear him! It's only given the police a perfect excuse to suspect your son-in-law of committing murder.' The grey eyes fastened on Gently. 'You don't

32

believe it, do you, George? You've talked to Hugh, you understand, this whole affair is quite preposterous. In the first place it was probably an accident, and in the second Hugh was somewhere else.'

Gently said nothing. Sir Charles peered in his glass. 'Hugh was in the forest, my dear,' he said.

'So what. He was in the forest! I could have been in the forest myself. I wasn't. We were riding by the old tank when we heard the shot back there. And Hugh was so far away, counting his caterpillars, that he didn't as much as hear it.'

'It was his gun.'

'And that's *quite* ridiculous! It could have been yours, or could have been mine.'

'But it happened to be his.'

'That's just my point. Why take his own gun, if he were going to shoot Laurie?'

Sir Charles shook his head, and drank. His wife stared anger at him, at Gently. Her lean cheeks were hot, and the glass in her hand trembled.

'In any case, it could have been a total outsider who sneaked in and borrowed a gun. It needn't have been to shoot Laurie. That could have been an accident. And then the fellow was too scared to own up.'

Gently said: 'But wasn't the gun-room locked?'

Lady Daphne and her husband exchanged glances. Sir Charles said: 'Yes, of course it was locked. At the same time, if somebody knew the ropes . . .'

'The – ropes?'

'Well . . .'

'Oh, I'll show him!' Lady Daphne said. 'He will want to go over the place sooner or later. You stay here, Charles. I'll see to it.'

She jumped up, and after a moment, Gently put down his glass and followed her. She led him back through the hall, down the steps, and then around the end of the house.

33

There they entered a paved stable-yard with a row of stalls and other outbuildings. Two horses poked their heads over the half-doors, to paw and whinny as they went by. Lady Daphne ignored them. She led Gently to the door of the adjacent tack-room.

'Now. The next door along is the gun-room. To go through that you need a key. But if the tack-room happens to be unlocked, well, then you don't need a key at all.'

She produced a key and unlocked the tack-room, which greeted them with an odour of leather and horse. At one end, on each side of a chimney-breast, were the doors of two full-length fitted cupboards. Lady Daphne threw open one of them. It was stuffed with liniments, oils and potions. She threw open the other. It revealed only vacant space, and the back of a similar door, beyond the chimney-breast. Lady Daphne wiggled through and pushed this door open. Gently followed; they stood in the gun-room.

'Do you understand now?'

Gently said: 'And – on Sunday?'

'On Sunday, of course, we didn't lock up! Would you have done, going off for a ride? I'm not sure we even shut the door.'

'And your son-in-law was helping you to saddle up?'

Her eyes were unfriendly. 'I won't deny it.'

'You rode off, leaving him here in the yard?'

'Oh no. He came out to see us off.'

'And . . . everything was left unlocked.'

'You bastard, George,' Lady Daphne said. 'The point is that just anyone at all could have got in here and taken a gun.'

'If they knew the way in.'

'If – if! More people use this way than the other. It isn't a secret, everyone knows it, it saves you going into the house for a key. So why must it be Hugh, and nobody else? Even an outsider could find his way through here.'

Gently shrugged, and glanced around the gun-room,

which was lit only dimly by a high, barred window; at the racked guns, the zinc-topped bench, the tools, pull-throughs, boxes of ammunition. Below the bench was a bin of spent cartridges, some of which had been matched to Merton's gun. But that proved nothing; any more than the positive paraffin test on his hands. Lady Daphne was watching him meanly.

'So?'

'Would you tell me just where you went riding, on Sunday?'

'Dear me, dear me!' She eyed him up and down, then turned with deliberation and squeezed back into the tack-room. Gently followed her, and into the yard. She locked the tack-room door emphatically.

'Well?'

She eyed him as though in amazement, and strode ahead of him back to the house.

There they found Sir Charles in the company of two other people, whom he hastened to introduce:

'Meet our resident author, Leslie Phipps, and our man with the camera, Dennys Brewster! I thought you would want a word with them, so I asked them to step in.'

Gently shook hands. Phipps was a smooth-faced, dark-haired man, with a goatee beard and supercilious eyes; Brewster a smiling, fair-haired fellow who grasped Gently's hand cordially. They were men in their fifties. Phipps was clad in a blazer, sported a flowing, fruity silk tie; Brewster in a baggy sports-jacket, and wearing no tie at all. He held on to Gently for a moment.

'Not sure that I can be much use to you!' he said. 'I didn't see anything, didn't hear anything. Most of the afternoon I was watching football, and before that I was in the library.'

'Would you have seen Timothy Stanton leaving with his stepbrother?'

'Oh – that!' Brewster grinned awkwardly at Sir Charles and Lady Daphne. 'Well, I suppose we all saw that. Timothy got up first, and a moment later Laurence jumped up and went after him. But that's all. Then I went into the library to look over some plates by the great Victorians. Then it was Italy versus Argentina in the TV lounge, with Sir Charles.'

Sir Charles made tutting noises. 'We don't have to hide anything!' he said. 'Timothy was making an ass of himself. He was rude to my secretary over lunch, and if Laurie hadn't put him right, then I would have done so. Nothing in that, just a personal matter. Nothing to do with what happened out there.'

'It might even have been Timothy putting Laurence right,' Lady Daphne said tartly. 'But of course, as you say, just a personal matter.'

Sir Charles threw her a look. Lady Daphne drifted over to the cabinet, where she poured herself a fresh drink.

'Well, then!' Sir Charles resumed. 'I didn't think Dennys could have much to tell you. And I, personally, can contribute nothing, since I spent the entire afternoon with the football. That leaves Leslie. Had it not been for him, this sad affair might not yet have come to light. For all anyone would have known, poor Laurie might just have taken himself off.'

Lady Daphne cleared her throat decorously. Phipps submitted a cool stare to Gently. Gently said:

'According to your statement, you spent the whole afternoon in the garden.'

'Until tea,' Phipps said. 'That is correct. In the garden settee, in the Round Garden. I had taken the papers and reviews down there. Also the proofs of an article for the *Guardian*.'

'From there, could you see the house?'

'No.'

'Would you have seen the ladies leaving for their ride?'

'I didn't see them, but I heard the hooves of their horses on the gravel, and the thud when they closed the gate.'

'Could you tell which direction they took?'

'To the best of my knowledge, towards the brecks.'

'Thank you, Leslie,' Lady Daphne said. 'Our new acquaintance *was* showing curiosity about that.'

Phipps shrugged, very faintly.

Gently said: 'And it was about then that you became aware of an altercation down at the moorings?'

'An altercation, yes. Though I couldn't distinguish what was being said. Then, it may have been ten minutes later, Laurence came stalking by. He passed through the garden, but completely ignored me.'

'He came from the moorings.'

'From that direction.'

'Going towards the forest?'

'Yes, towards the forest. He took the path through the shrubberies, and I heard the gate thud again.'

'And – the gate thudded a third time?'

Phipps nodded slowly. 'Ten minutes or so after that. But of course, I can't tell you who it was. Just that I heard the thud of the gate.'

'Oh, what is the point of all this!' Lady Daphne exclaimed. 'We know that Hugh was going out just then. So what does it prove? Just that Hugh told the truth, that he went about his business the way he said. There's no mystery. If Laurence was shot, it was some stupid accident, and that's all. And poor Hugh just happened to be out there, half a mile away, looking after his trees.'

'Oh, come now, Daphne!' her husband protested. 'These things have to be asked, you know. It isn't just a dispute about who's bird, or of someone's dog being peppered.' He turned apologetically to Gently. 'You will have to allow for us,' he said. 'We are all still a little upset by this. Had you any more questions to put to these gentlemen?'

Gently shook his head. 'Not immediately, but I would like to have a word with your son.'

'With Timothy?'

'If I may.'

'Ah.' Sir Charles looked thoughtful. 'Well, you will probably find him at the moorings. One of these gentlemen will point out the way. But please don't run off, will you? We shall be having tea in half an hour.'

Gently promised he wouldn't run off. Lady Daphne's expression was perhaps less than hospitable. Phipps fingered his beard, and dropped into a chair. It was the smiling Brewster who showed Gently his path.

3

The path to the moorings, a rough track, departed from the drive not far from the house; but before Gently could embark on it he saw Calthorpe's Escort approaching. He signalled; Calthorpe pulled over, and Gently got in beside him. The local man was in a state of excitement.

'Sir – we got hold of that Robinson fellow! Bodney called at the Forestry Centre, and picked him up straight away.'

'So what does he say?'

'That report, sir. Robinson put it in a fortnight ago. And the gist of it is that section 10 was healthy, with only marginal infection, which he'd already dealt with.'

'Robinson had dealt with it?'

'Yes, sir. Gives section 10 a clean bill of health. So like that there wasn't any need for Merton to go checking it on a Sunday.'

'Have you put it to Merton?'

'No, sir. I thought I'd better report it to you.'

'It could have been genuine. A conscientious forestry officer on a follow-up inspection.'

'But on a Sunday afternoon, sir?'

'Perhaps. If he had nothing better to do.'

Calthorpe shook his head decidedly. 'No, sir. I can't go along with that. Not when chummie is looking for an excuse as hard as Merton is looking for one. He was out there when Stanton was shot, it was his gun, and we can show motive. So he's got to give out he was somewhere else, and this is the best he could come up with. And I reckon it isn't good enough, sir, not however conscientious he might be.'

Gently felt for his pipe. 'Yet we still need a witness ... someone who can place him right there, in that dell.'

'Won't be easy, sir,' Calthorpe said. 'They don't grow on trees, in a situation like that.'

'Not on trees. But how about horses?'

'Horses ...?' Calthorpe turned to stare at Gently.

'Horses certainly pass there.' Gently pondered on the pipe. 'And someone I talked to wasn't very forthcoming.'

'You mean – ?'

'Lady Daphne.'

'Oh lor'!' Calthorpe said. 'You don't really think she's tied up in it, sir?'

Gently said: 'She may have seen something. And that something she isn't prepared to tell.'

'She – saw Merton.'

'That's possible. And if so, she is never going to admit it. On the other hand ...'

'Sir?'

Gently shrugged, and put away the pipe. 'Let's get this vehicle parked! Then we'll go and chat with a man on a houseboat.'

Calthorpe parked obsequiously on a corner of the sweep, remote from the house and the other cars; then they set off along the track which, dipping steeply through a stand of trees, soon brought them to low, marshy ground and the reeded bank of the river. A final turn revealed a piled staithe with a long, white houseboat moored to it; it also revealed a flush-faced Cassandra Merton glaring at a pale-haired young man in sweat-shirt and jeans. They both jerked round as the policemen approached, Cassandra Merton with her chin stuck out.

'Oh – so you've got round to Timothy! I wondered how long it was going to take you. Well, you're welcome to him. Have fun! A shame if my brother missed out on the Gestapo.'

'Mrs Merton – '

'Don't waste your charm. Not while you've still got Hugh in a cell.'

'If I might have a word – '

'Get lost, copper. When I want a word with you, I'll let you know.'

And she marched past them, head in the air, pausing only to feint a spit. Timothy Stanton edged forward uncertainly, tried to muster an apologetic grin.

'Don't mind her – it's just her way! She's been like that since she was a kid.'

Tall, slim, in his late twenties, he had soft brown eyes in a fine-featured face.

'So what was that all about?'

'Nothing at all. She's just trying to get dear Hugh off the hook. And you shouldn't pay too much attention to what she says. Cassie has always been an accomplished fibber.'

'But she thinks you might help her?'

'Well, I can't! I'm not telling stories for her or anyone.'

'Stories?'

'Oh, never mind! Let's pretend that's something I never said.' He found up another grin. 'So you're Gently, the ogre my sister was telling me about. Well, well. You look quite civilized. Perhaps I should even invite you aboard.'

Gently stared at him. Timothy Stanton stared back. There was something almost feminine in his smooth features. He wore his hair in a shoulder-brushing nest, and had a gold ring in one of his ears. He indicated the houseboat.

'Well . . . shall we?'

He stood aside to let them clamber aboard. The after part of the houseboat was roofed, but not cabined, and was

41

furnished with a table and four wicker chairs. There stood also an easel, and on a stool beside it a palette, brushes and dipper. On the easel rested a partly finished canvas, while a glance into the cabin revealed other paintings, clearly from the same brush. Timothy Stanton waved them to chairs. Before sitting himself, he struck a critical attitude before the easel.

'A shade more brio in the browns, would you say?'

Gently didn't say anything.

'Do forgive me,' Timothy Stanton said. 'But painting is the *raison d'être* of these parts. If you've been to the house you'll understand. Everyone there lives classical painting. Father lavishes his ill-gotten wealth on it, Mother arranges exhibitions, Leslie compiles massive tomes about it and Dennys takes endless photographs. It's almost obscene. It becomes just one of us to let in a breath of fresh air. I'm not exactly a modernist, as you can see, but nobody could accuse me of being classical.'

'You are a professional painter?' Gently said.

'Don't be naughty!' Timothy Stanton said. 'But yes, I do sell a canvas now and then, when Mother fixes me up a show.'

'You make a living from it?'

'Oh Leonardo, forgive him!' Timothy Stanton sighed. 'I fear me I have fallen among the Philistines. And yet, you have a sympathetic face. No, not yet. I don't make a living. But doubtless fame will come in good time. And who knows, I may sell even you a canvas, a sweet breath of Eden to take back to London.'

Carelessly, he dropped on a chair, grinned at Gently, grinned at Calthorpe. Yet was he really so much at ease as his manner sought to convey? His eyes were evasive, now met yours, now switched to the easel, to the river bank. His sandalled foot scuffed against a chair-leg, he let one of his hands hang, swinging. Gently said:

42

'And your stepbrother – was he also enthusiastic about painting?'

'Laurie? You jest, kind sir. Laurie wouldn't have known a Turner from a Van Gogh.'

'He was what you would call a Philistine?'

'In capital letters. Laurie was fresh out of the bush. I suppose I mustn't speak evil of the dead, but even his books proclaimed him a moron.'

'In short, you didn't like him.'

'In short. Just in passing, I didn't shoot him, either. I spent the livelong Sunday afternoon where I'm sitting now, listening to tapes. That's what I told your friend, and that's what I'm telling you.'

'After he left, you sat playing tapes.'

'Elgar and Britten, to be precise.'

'The whole afternoon.'

'*Si.*' But now the swinging hand had ceased to swing.

Gently said: 'If you don't mind, we will go back to that lunch on Sunday. I understand there was some unpleasantness. Involving yourself and your father's secretary.'

'How nicely you put it,' Timothy Stanton said. 'I believe I did pass some observation. Like calling Emma a scheming bitch, it may even have been something stronger. Have you met her?'

Gently said nothing.

'Just your average p.s.,' Timothy Stanton said. 'Younger than some. More comely than some. But just a p.s., when all's said and done.'

Gently said: 'Hadn't she been your mistress?'

'Oh, I do like that,' Timothy Stanton said. 'Now you're going out of your way to flatter me. If only I could truthfully answer yes.'

'She wasn't?'

'She wasn't.'

'But you would have liked her to be.'

43

Timothy Stanton regarded the river bank. 'Of course. I'm young,' he said. 'And male. And one of those naughty creatures, a painter. And Emma Spinks wasn't fixed up. And not at all backward in fielding woo.' His mouth grinned, but his eyes didn't.

'In so many words, you didn't score.'

'If you say so.'

'Then, into the picture, stepped this husky relative from down-under.'

'Into the picture,' Timothy Stanton said. 'Almost, you're speaking my language.'

'Who had better success with Miss Spinks.'

'I love it so much,' Timothy Stanton said.

'Well?'

He swung his hand. Now even his mouth wasn't grinning.

'At Sunday lunch, you made this remark, which resulted in your stepbrother following you down here.'

'Brotherly love,' Timothy Stanton said. 'He wished me to clarify my statement.' He gazed at the bank. 'He was sitting with Emma. Or it may have been Emma was sitting with him. Anyway their heads were together, and probably their feet under the table. He asked her what she was doing after lunch. She told him she was going to walk the dogs. He asked if he could go too. She said yes. Then I made my modest contribution. And rose. And left.'

'And – he followed.'

A swing of the hand. 'Indeed, we had quite a conversation. He offered me a minute analysis of my character, and I replied with a minute analysis of his. Then the discussion turned to Emma, Miss Spinks. I believe I enlightened him on one or two points. He seemed to have difficulty in comprehending me, and our exchanges became more emphatic.'

'In fact, blows were struck.'

'Fraternal gestures.' Timothy Stanton touched a cheek,

where a faint blueness yet lingered. 'Soon after which we expressed mutual farewells, and he departed in the direction of the forest.'

'And you sat down. And played tapes.'

'It seemed the most restful thing to do.'

'While you nursed your bruises.'

'Mere trifles. In fact, I opened a can of beer.'

'And here you remained.'

'Exactly here.'

Gently stared at him for a moment. 'Then a witness who saw you in some other place must, of necessity, have been mistaken.'

Timothy Stanton's eyes hit his. His mouth had fallen, very slightly, open.

'Who says that?'

'Would it be true?'

'What I'm asking is, who told you!'

'Does it matter?'

'Yes, it does!'

'Then shall we say a member of your family?'

Timothy Stanton's eyes were large, the brows lifting; his lips were still parted over even white teeth. He struck the table.

'Cassandra, wasn't it? She'd tell any lie to get Hugh off! Well, it won't work, and you can tell her from me. I'm not playing games to suit my sister.'

'Could she have seen you?'

'No, she couldn't. She was riding with Mother, on the brecks.'

'On the skirts of the forest.'

'So there you are. She wasn't down here, and she couldn't have seen me.'

'Could anyone?'

45

A hesitation! 'They would have to have come down here, wouldn't they?'

'But no one did?'

'No!'

Gently shrugged. 'Then we have only your word that you remained here, haven't we?'

'My . . . what?'

'Your account lacks confirmation. And you were the second last person to see your stepbrother alive.'

The staring eyes were painful; and there was fear in them. But slowly, so slowly, they began to relax. The hand that had tensed swung free again, the ghost of a grin crept back to the mouth.

'You, you really are an expert, aren't you?'

Gently watched, but said nothing.

'I'm beginning to understand why they called you in! You can make even an innocent like me feel guilty. But you're wrong, you know, quite wrong. I really did spend the afternoon here. And I wasn't the second last person to see Laurie alive. You're forgetting the naughty boy who shot him.'

Gently stared, then pointed to the bank. 'In the garden, your stepbrother passed Mr Phipps. Mr Phipps heard the field-gate thud as your brother passed through it. Then, after an interval, he heard it thud again.'

'Dear sir, and if he did?'

Gently nodded to the trees. 'There is access to the house without going through the garden.'

'Access . . . you mean, I could have been the thudder?'

'The timing suggests that possibility.'

'Oh, souls of poets!' But the grin had gone again. 'Yes, I can see it all now. There I go, crossed in love, determined to take a bloody revenge. Up to the house. Into the gun-room. I would pick on dear Hugh's weapon, of course. And through the gate in my manic rage, heartily thudding it as I went. Is that the picture?'

46

Gently was silent.

'Of course, it needs touching up,' Timothy Stanton said. 'I think I might have stopped that gate from thudding, if I were going to stalk someone in the forest. And I would have donned my coat of invisibility, in case I ran into someone at the house. But apart from that, no problem. When the timing suggests the possibility.'

Gently said: 'Do you have a key to the gun-room?'

'Sorry, so sorry,' Timothy Stanton said. 'No, I don't. I would have to have fetched one. I would have had to apply to Father.'

'Even – when the tack-room door was unlocked?'

'The – tack-room?'

Gently nodded. Again, the stare, the fear: the hand arrested in its swing. Then, the recovery.

'Ah me, these professionals! And for a moment there, I thought I had you. Of course, you are absolutely right. With the horses out, who would need a key?'

Now it was Calthorpe who was staring. 'I don't quite get this, sir,' he said.

'You wouldn't,' Timothy Stanton said. 'It's too stalky. It takes a name from the Yard to spot these things.'

Gently explained. Calthorpe looked grim.

'So like that, sir, it could have been anyone?'

'Anyone who knew the back way in.'

'Isn't it unfortunate,' Timothy Stanton said. 'You know, it needn't even have been old Hugh.'

Calthorpe glared at him. Timothy Stanton grinned back. Then he caught Gently's eye, and looked away. Gently said:

'Adding everything together, it seems unfortunate that we can't confirm your movements. You had access to the weapon, opportunity, and were fresh from a violent quarrel with the deceased. Have you anything to add?'

Timothy Stanton turned his eyes up. 'Just that I love you for trying it on. But of course, it doesn't really add up to anything, because I was here listening to my Elgar and Britten.'

'After such an encounter?'

'I *like* Elgar. Though I'm not so sure about Britten and Pearsy. But yes, in small doses. Then there's Holst. I can take him.'

Gently said: 'This is a serious matter.'

'So is Holst,' Timothy Stanton said.

'And that's all you have to say?'

'Why not? Since clearly you don't have a leg to stand on.'

Gently said: 'Then, in that case, you won't mind accompanying this officer to the police station. He will be requiring you to take a test to show if you have recently discharged a gun.'

Timothy Stanton's hand stopped dead: once more, his lips were slowly gaping.

'But that's unfair. I won't do it! You're simply trying to hang something on me.'

'You have some objection?'

'Yes! This is nothing but police harassment.'

'Now, come along, sir,' Calthorpe said, rising. 'This won't hurt you. Just a simple little test.'

'But listen – listen! How long ago can this test show I was using a gun?'

'How long, sir?'

'Yes, how long! Because last week – Saturday – I was taking a pot at the squirrels.'

Gently and Calthorpe exchanged glances. 'On Saturday, you say, sir?' Calthorpe said.

'Yes, Saturday.'

'Well, there you are, sir. But I still think you'd better come along.'

'But I'm admitting it – I used a gun on Saturday!'

'Then we'll have to see what we find, sir.'

'You'll pretend it was Sunday!'

48

'Just a test, sir,' Calthorpe said. 'It won't take long. I've got my car here.'

Timothy Stanton's eyes darted to the bank, and for a moment it seemed he might attempt to run for it. But the sturdy figure of Calthorpe interposed, and Timothy Stanton remained in his chair.

'Shall we go, sir?'

'Very well, then! Play this stupid farce if you have to. But it isn't going to prove a thing, except that I shot a squirrel on Saturday.'

'So then you've nothing to worry about, sir.'

'No, but you may have, when I tell my father!'

'If you'll just come along, sir.'

Timothy Stanton glared at him. But got to his feet.

For some minutes longer Gently remained on the houseboat, brooding over the canvases that adorned the cabin. Strangely, they offered a mixture of precise realism with an impressionism that seemed almost to have gone mad. The canvas on the easel was typical. It appeared to be the prospect from the well of the houseboat. In islands of near-photographic detail were portrayed the rushes, some meadow-sweet and six crowns of hemp-agrimony. But the rest was a shambles, crude slabs of raw colour, barely linked to the view of river, reeds, and the lowering roof of the houseboat. A picture unfinished? But no; those hanging in the cabin followed the same scheme, the same intemperate brushwork mingling with vignettes of intense realism. As a manner, it defied a label. And probably defied customers as well.

'Hullo – are you there?'

The houseboat lurched as someone stepped aboard. A moment later the photographer, Brewster, climbed down into the well.

'They sent me to fetch you to tea ... I ran into your

colleague in the drive! It was rather alarming, he was carting off Timothy. You don't mean to lock him up too, do you?'

'Just a routine matter.'

'Well, if you say so! He probably wouldn't have come in to tea, anyway. Too bourgeois. As I dare say you noticed, Timothy aims to be an artist to his fingertips.' Brewster gave Gently a conspiratorial smile. 'So what do you make of our young genius's pictures? Not exactly Gainsborough or Constable, are they? What do you say to Neo-Schizophrenic?'

Gently stared. 'Is he schizophrenic?'

'Oh lord, no! I'm merely talking of the pictures. His contrast of Look At This and You Go To Hell. I suppose it just could be the next movement in art.'

'Is that the intention?'

'What else? Though it hasn't quite hit the headlines yet. But he does have his mother behind him, and she is a very formidable lady.'

'What about his father?'

Brewster mimed a double-take. 'If it's later than Munnings, it doesn't interest Sir Charles! Until Timothy paints him, shall we say, a pseudo-Constable, Sir Charles probably thinks he's wasting his time.'

He took a stance before the canvas on the easel that was not unlike that of Timothy Stanton's. Then he hissed through his teeth, and shook his head; gave Gently a sly look.

Gently said: 'Were you down here on Saturday?'

'Oh, I was here all the week,' Brewster said. 'This is quite a business, this book of Leslie's. I've had to set up a darkroom and really move in.'

'On the Saturday, what were people doing?'

'On the Saturday?' Brewster's eyes narrowed. 'As far as I remember, Sir Charles and Lady Daphne took their

50

daughter into Latchford, shopping. But I was away myself. I had to skip back to town to pick up a fresh supply of film.'

'And the others?'

'I wouldn't know. I dare say our Aussie friend went along with the others. I believe Merton had to call in at the Forestry Centre. And doubtless Leslie was bashing his typewriter.'

'And Timothy Stanton?'

'You'd have to ask him. Oh dear!' Brewster's eyes were shrewd. 'That's what you're really after, isn't it? You're still on the trail of our tame genius.'

'Well?'

Brewster shook his head. 'As I said, you'd have to ask him. But a tenner on it he was down here, probably painting this ridiculous picture. But ... you aren't serious, are you?'

'Merely routine.'

Brewster looked away 'I don't like the sound of it.'

'You are a friend of his?'

'Let's say he amuses me. And I'm damned certain you're on the wrong track.'

Gently shrugged at the easel. 'In that case, we had better be getting up to tea! Perhaps you'll show me the route through the Round Garden, if it won't take us very much longer.'

Brewster gave him a stare, then stepped ashore. He led them a few yards up the bank. From there, a track skirted an area of soggy marsh to approach a screen of rhododendrons at a higher level. Then, within a hundred yards of the mooring, they entered a small formal garden, completely surrounded by beech hedging, with paths leading off in two directions. A pond formed the central feature. Beside it stood a garden swing-settee. Just the roof of the house showed in the distance, and tall trees beyond the hedging offered dappled shade. Gently paused a moment;

51

Brewster kept staring at him. At last he gave Gently a rueful grin.

'Listen! If it's the least bit of good, I can probably go bail for Timothy. I can't say where he was at the time of the shooting, but he was up at the house at around three.'

Gently's expression was strictly neutral. 'You can place him at the house?'

'Absolutely. He'd come up to fill those water-containers he has on the houseboat.'

'And you spoke to him?'

'I didn't say that! No, I saw him go by the library window. He was carrying the two containers, and I had my eye on the time because of the football.'

'He'd be going through to the kitchen?'

'No, of course not. There's a tap the gardener uses.'

'And you saw him returning, with the full containers?'

'Well, I must admit . . . yes! I did catch a glimpse of him.'

Gently set the swing-settee swinging. He said: 'Mr Brewster, I think you are lying.'

'No, but really!'

'You didn't see Timothy Stanton. Either around three or at any other time.'

'Well, if you don't believe me – '

'I don't believe you.'

Brewster drew himself up in mock indignation. He said: 'Well, that's a fine way to treat a member of the Addlestone Photographic Society! But just between you and me – if you like, between you and me and that damned settee . . .'

'Yes?'

'Can you honestly believe that our sainted Timothy would have had the nerve?'

Gently was prevented from replying by a sudden rustle on the path from the house, and a wrathful Cassandra Merton emerged to plant herself before them.

'Great bustards, what's keeping you?' she exclaimed. 'Mother is waiting to pour tea!' Then, her eye flitting round the garden, 'But where's Timothy? What have you done with him?'

'Better ask our new friend!' Brewster smirked.

Cassandra Merton fastened her eye on Gently. Gently said:

'Your brother is attending to a matter at the police station. He is unlikely to be detained.'

'But – you've run him in?'

'He was driven to the police station.'

'You know what I mean! He's on your list.'

'He is simply assisting with some routine, and will be returning here later.'

Her lively eyes were relishing, and something else was on the tip of her tongue. But she didn't speak it. Instead, she made shooing motions towards the house.

'For glory's sake, get a move on! Jenny brought in the tea quarter of an hour ago. And if there was one thing Daddy learned at the Treasury, it was to expect to have his tea served on the very dot.'

4

'No Timothy?'

Along with others in the lounge was a robust-figured, sad-faced girl, who was assisting the maid, Jenny, in handing round the cups and plates. Lady Daphne was seated on the sofa, where her daughter promptly joined her; Phipps sat by the window; after a moment's hesitation, Brewster had selected a chair across the room from him. Sir Charles was standing before the hearth, above which hung a painting of horses with a groom, an undoubted Morland.

'Isn't he coming, then?'

Cassandra Merton tittered. 'You'll never see Timothy again, Daddy! They carried him off, screaming. Apparently he was in it along with Hugh.'

'Be quiet, you silly girl.'

'Well, why not? It's just as credible. In fact, I should say even more so. You know how Timothy loves to show off.'

'Stop behaving like an idiot.'

'Oh, dear me. But they've got him, Daddy. They've banged him up.'

'Is this true?' Sir Charles asked Gently.

Gently accepted his cup from the sad-faced girl. 'Your son is at the police station on a routine matter. He is certainly not under arrest.'

'That's what they always say,' Cassandra Merton jeered. 'That's what they said when they grabbed Hugh. A routine

54

matter. And Hugh is still down there. Better face it, Daddy. We've lost Timothy.'

Sir Charles threw her a look. 'Are we allowed to know what business the police have with my son?'

'Yes – what's the idea?' Lady Daphne demanded. 'Why have you carted him off without a word to anyone?'

Gently sipped tea. He said: 'In brief, your son is undergoing a certain test. It is to confirm whether or not he has recently discharged a firearm.' He paused. 'I may add to that a statement from him that he used a gun on Saturday, and that it would be of assistance to us if we could have his statement confirmed.'

All of them were staring at him.

'Wow!' Brewster murmured. 'And you're telling us he isn't under arrest?'

'He is helping us to establish a fact.'

'But what a fact!' Brewster said.

Sir Charles was frowning. 'Of course, I appreciate the need for this,' he said. 'But at the same time I would point out that guns are in frequent use with us. We all shoot. Game is out of season, but there are plenty of vermin to keep our hands in. The brecks are infested with rabbits, and grey squirrels have taken over our trees.'

'I can't believe this!' Lady Daphne exclaimed. 'Good lord, there's scarcely a day goes by. Everyone takes a pot at the bunnies. You could test me positive for a start.'

'Everyone . . . ?'

'Yes, everyone.' She cast a glance at Jenny. 'Not the servants, of course. But everyone else. We keep a couple of spare guns. In a place like this it's the way of life.'

'Your guests too?'

'Our guests too.'

'Count me in,' Brewster grinned. 'I've had a crack. And I've seen old Les coming back with a bunny.'

'This was – recently?'

'Friday, wasn't it?'

Leslie Phipps didn't look amused.

'Yes, Friday,' Brewster said. 'I remember now. And he gave the bunny to the gardener.'

'So now you know,' Lady Daphne said. 'It would be a strange thing if Timothy hadn't used a gun lately. And if he says he used one on Saturday, what reason in the world is there for not believing him?'

But Sir Charles was still frowning. 'This test,' he said. 'For what period of time might it be valid?'

'For four days.'

'For four days.'

Brewster grinned at Phipps, who stared back thunderously.

Sir Charles said: 'Yes. I do take the point. You require confirmation if that is at all possible. Unfortunately, on Saturday, most of us were away from the house. Were you at home, Emma?'

'No, Sir Charles. No.' The sad-faced girl shook her head. She faced Gently with fluttering eyes. 'I drove over to Abbotsham to visit my parents.'

'What about you, Jenny?'

'Oh no, sir!'

'You didn't hear any shooting?'

'Not me, sir.'

'That seems to leave you, Leslie,' Sir Charles said to Phipps. 'I believe you were here all day, weren't you?'

'Indeed I was.' Phipps gave Brewster a last disparaging stare. 'I spent an occupational day. I was writing my reviews in the study. Jenny was kind enough to bring me lunch, which I ate in the TV lounge, watching rubbish. Then I returned to professional duties. Of your son Timothy I saw nothing till dinner.'

'So you can't help us.'

'I didn't say that.' Phipps took a delicate sip of tea. 'It would be mid-afternoon, I suppose, say between half-past three and four. I was appraising a gentleman by the name

56

of Fanshawe, who has some quite absurd ideas about Vermeer, when the trend of my observations was interrupted. In effect, I heard a couple of shots.'

'You did!'

Phipps nodded. 'In the general direction of the river. Rather faint and far away. But of course, I am unable to say who fired them.'

'Timothy – it would have to be Timothy.'

Phipps inclined his head. 'If you say so.' He looked bored. Emma Spinks, Gently noticed, was regarding him with an odd intentness.

'So that's it,' Sir Charles said. 'There's confirmation for you, George.'

'Oh, hoots!' Cassandra Merton exclaimed. 'I did so want dear Timothy to be under suspicion too.'

'It's nonsense, all of it,' her mother said. 'This whole business, first to last. Nobody intended any harm to Laurence, that's getting plainer all the time.'

Sir Charles gave Gently a steady look. 'That expresses the consensus of opinion here,' he said. 'At first sight it looked like something dastardly, but the more you mull it over, the more doubtful it gets. Accidents with guns certainly happen. It takes only a stumble, or something catching in a trigger. Then the shock of having done such a thing, in this instance, might well have caused the culprit to decide to lie low. Wouldn't you agree?'

Gently said nothing.

'Additionally, it didn't have to be one of us.'

'Of course it didn't!' Lady Daphne weighed in. 'Any prowler could have got at those guns. Just suppose one did, and he met up with Laurence, and there was an accident. Would you expect him to report it? Then, of course, he wouldn't dare to keep the gun, so what would be the safest thing to do with it? Why, put it back from where he'd taken it, and shift any blame on to us.'

'Yes – that's a possibility,' Sir Charles kept his eye on Gently. 'Something like that might very well explain it. At least you may think it equally credible with a deliberate crime by one of the household.'

'For instance, Hugh,' Cassandra Merton said bitingly. 'Though you can play games with Timothy, and welcome.'

'Hush, girl!' Sir Charles said. 'But isn't it a possibility to be kept in mind?'

Gently stared, very slowly shook his head.

'Oh, come on, be a sport!' Brewster murmured.

Sir Charles and his lady exchanged glances; then the latter shrugged faintly. She turned to the maid.

'Jenny, hand those cakes round! And pour some fresh tea before it gets quite cold.'

Somewhere distant, a telephone rang. Emma Spinks jumped up and ran to attend to it. Shortly, she returned. She looked at Gently.

'It's for you . . .'

She led him down the hall to what was probably the study, a spacious room with a massive desk, and hung, like every-where else he had seen, with row upon row of paintings. Having shown him in, she retreated, but only as far as the door. Gently ignored her and picked up the phone, seated himself on the luxurious desk-chair.

'Calthorpe, sir . . . that test was positive. Are we going to believe what he tells us about Saturday?'

Gently grunted. 'I've found a witness – of a sort! There's half a chance he was telling half the truth.'

'Oh dear, sir! Do I turn him loose?'

'Before you do that, put him on.'

Emma Spinks still hovered by the door, and Gently still continued to ignore her. On the desk was a typewriter with a sheet in it. Gently drew it towards him: it was a piece about Samuel Palmer.

'Here's Stanton, sir.'

From the corner of his eye, Gently could see Emma Spinks edging closer.

'Stanton?'

'Yes, and I'd like to tell you – '

'I hear your test was positive, Stanton.'

'All right, I've admitted all that! And you've got no reason – '

'Let's talk about Sunday.'

'Sunday – what about Sunday?'

'When your stepbrother left you at the houseboat.'

'Listen – !'

'When you were feeling thirsty, no doubt, and went to get a drink from one of the containers.'

'One of the containers – what – ?'

Still Emma Spinks was edging closer.

'One of those containers you keep on the houseboat – where do you fill them? In the stable-yard?'

'Look, I don't know what this is about – !'

'Didn't you fill your containers on Sunday?'

'No, I didn't – and I don't fill them there!'

'Not the stable-yard?'

'I simply didn't!'

'You simply didn't.' Casually, Gently caught Emma Spinks's wretched gaze. 'Then someone who thought they saw you was mistaken – on Sunday afternoon, with your containers?'

'Yes – they damned well were!'

'With or without them?'

'I never, never left the houseboat!'

'Thank you,' Gently said. 'Stanton. Would you put Inspector Calthorpe back on?'

A pause of some moments. Then Calthorpe:

'So what was all that about, sir!'

Gently shrugged at Emma Spinks. 'Call it an alibi that never was.'

'An alibi – for young Stanton, sir?'

'Remind me to tell you about it later. But for now, you'd better show him the door.'

'Yes, sir. And I shan't be sorry to do that.'

Gently hung up. He adjusted the typewriter. He looked encouragingly at Emma Spinks. Emma Spinks stared miserably at Gently. Then she flopped on a chair and burst into tears.

'It's all my fault!'

She had found a handkerchief, and now was sobbing into that. A crumpled figure, she was hugging a chair a little to the side of the big desk. Briefly, a figure had appeared at the door, and Sir Charles's concerned gaze had taken in the scene; then, at a gesture from Gently, he had silently withdrawn, closing the door after him.

'I led Timothy on, I don't deny it. But I never thought he really cared! It was only a silly game. He wanted to *believe* he was in love with me. And now – ' sobs choked her for a moment – 'now this terrible thing has happened. And I'm to blame. I couldn't help it. From the moment Laurie walked in through the door . . .'

To the typewriter, Gently said: 'If it is any comfort, I think you summed up Timothy Stanton correctly.'

'But I led him on! I let him think I believed it, and that I had fallen in love with him.'

'In fact, a silly game.'

'Yes, a game. Timothy wants so much to be romantic. And I played it too. It was fun. How could I know it would end like this?'

'You couldn't, of course.'

'But it's all my fault! When Laurie came along I just fell. I carried on as though Timothy didn't exist. I didn't care if it hurt him or not.' She sobbed. 'And it did hurt him. That's the beastly thing about it. And now – now – I

60

heard you on the phone! You seemed so certain that Timothy did it.'

Gently said: 'Perhaps you're jumping to conclusions.'

'No. I heard you. All about his alibi. And why would he need an alibi, unless you think he's the one you're after?'

Gently shook his head. 'That was routine. We have to check the information people give us.'

'But it wasn't just a check – you were trying to trap him!'

'Sometimes people are reluctant to help us.'

She scrubbed at her eyes, then turned her face to him. She had pretty, heart-shaped features. Her light brown hair was cut short and businesslike, and she had appealing hazel eyes. She stuffed the handkerchief in the sleeve of her blouse.

'It wasn't Timothy. I'm certain it wasn't. After the row he would just have been shattered. They had a fight, did you know that? I nearly went back to comfort Timothy.'

Gently stared. 'Then you were there?'

'No! I kept well clear of the moorings. I hurried by as quickly as I could, but I could hear it going on.'

'I see.' Gently kept staring. 'Perhaps we should go back to what happened at lunch.'

'Oh, that.' She tossed her head feebly. 'Well, Timothy said something very, very rude. I think even Laurie was shocked. He sat still for a while after Timothy stalked out. Then he jumped up and excused himself and took off after Timothy.'

'And you?'

'I was so ashamed! I didn't know where to put myself. In the end I excused myself too, and called the dogs, and went.'

'But . . . towards the moorings?'

'No – yes. At least, I didn't meant to go that way! But I couldn't help it. And there's a track to the river that goes close by, without actually coming out on the moorings.'

'So you heard them rowing.'

She nodded. 'I'd got the dogs on the lead by then.'

'And – the fight?'

'When I heard them getting so angry I was scared and hurried away. I was actually running! I could hear someone's face slapped, and Laurie shouting he wouldn't take that from a whingeing pom. Of course, he was bigger and stronger than Timothy. I knew that Timothy would come off worst.'

'But you didn't go back.'

'I was scared. Don't forget it was me the trouble was about. So I ran and kept running. At least the dogs were enjoying themselves.'

'Where did you run to?'

'Oh, up the river bank. There's a walk that goes on for miles.'

'On the edge of the brecks?'

'More or less. But there's marsh and scrub in between.'

'You wouldn't have seen the horsewomen?'

'Oh no.'

'Or anyone?'

She shook her head. 'I probably walked a couple of miles, and then came back the same way. That's when I thought of going to cheer up Timothy. But in the end I just went back to the house.'

'It was all quiet at the moorings.'

Her hazel eyes fixed him. 'But Timothy was there. I'll swear he was. And he came up to tea later.'

'You didn't hear him, say, playing taped music?'

'He was there. And that's that.'

'Can you estimate the time?'

'Yes. Around four. I had time to wash and tidy before tea.'

Then, for some reason, she glanced at the door, which Sir Charles had so carefully and softly closed. She hitched her

chair closer to the desk, fixed her eyes yet more firmly on
Gently.

'Perhaps I shouldn't be telling you this, and if you
weren't so rotten about Timothy perhaps I wouldn't. But
there's another member of the household who deserves to
be getting a bit of your attention.' She reached across and
touched the paper in the typewriter. 'And he's rather
proud of his prowess with a gun.'

'We are talking of Mr Phipps?'

She nodded, gave another hasty glance to the door. 'I
may be putting my job in jeopardy, but someone should be
giving you the whole picture.'

'There is something I should know?'

'There certainly is. And I am the person who can tell you.
You won't be getting it from Sir Charles, and I doubt if he's
mentioned it to anyone else.'

'Touching . . . Mr Phipps?'

'Oh yes. Our resident celebrity, Mr Phipps. Our authority on classical landscape. The biographer of Constable.
Mr Phipps.'

Gently gave her a stare. 'Go on.'

One more glance at the door! 'Right. So Laurie was an
author too, wasn't he? And one quite as famous as Mr
Phipps.'

'You wouldn't be suggesting professional jealousy?'

She shook her head impatiently. 'More than that. It was
his book that was at stake, the book he's doing on Sir
Charles's collection. He's been on it now for weeks, and
then suddenly this author son turns up – quite capable, his
father thinks, of doing the book himself. *The Stanton Collection*, by Laurence Stanton. You can see how it would
appeal.'

'But . . . if Mr Phipps was already engaged on it?'

63

'Sir Charles was ready to pay him off. I'm not sure that Laurie wanted the job, but he was prepared to go along. Sir Charles was obsessed with keeping Laurie here, he had already offered him Bracken Brae. The book would have been a clincher. It would probably have meant Laurie staying on for good.'

Gently went on staring. 'And . . . Mr Phipps?'

Emma Spinks made a little face. 'I was here when it was hinted to him. He kept his temper with Sir Charles, but only with the greatest effort. He pointed out in his snide way that Laurie was merely a writer of sensational fiction, while he was quoted as a world authority on the subject of classical landscape. He wouldn't even consider a joint production, which was another idea of Sir Charles's. Sir Charles was diplomatic, of course. But you could see that the notion wasn't going to go away.'

'It was left hanging over Mr Phipps's head.'

'Yes, it was. And it was plain that he knew it. He sulked about like a great child, and cut Laurie completely dead.'

'And – this would be a motive for what happened on Sunday?'

'He was the last person to see Laurie alive, wasn't he?'

'He would have gone to that length?'

'Why not? And I can tell you this. He wasn't where he says he was on Sunday.'

Now Gently was really staring! 'So where do you say he was, Miss Spinks?'

'I don't know, do I? But he wasn't in the garden. Not when I came back with the dogs.'

'You didn't see him at all?'

'No. Not in the garden, not in the house. So he is at least as suspect as Timothy, when you start lining people up.'

Gently shook his head. 'I shall have to bear that in mind! And this is the extent of your information?'

Emma Spinks eyed him bitterly; she shut her mouth tight. Then she jumped up from her chair, and flounced out of the room. Gently followed. In the hall he came face to face with Sir Charles.

Also in the hall was the maid, Jenny, who was carefully stacking crockery on a tea-trolley; Sir Charles glanced towards her, then signed to Gently to follow him. They passed through glazed double doors at the top of the hall into a vast, gloomy room, lit only by panes in a roof that arched at least thirty feet above them. Sir Charles operated switches. Lights flashed in a row of chandeliers. Then you saw you were in a handsome gallery, its walls lined to capacity with gilt-framed paintings. Of their quality there could be no doubt. The eye drifted from Morland to Wilson and Crome. Finally, it came to rest on a majestic Constable, in a place of honour, facing the doors. The only furniture was back-to-back benches occupying the centre of the floor; but high in each corner Gently could observe the camera eyes of a security system. Sir Charles gave him a conspiratorial look.

'Never fear! I had Treasury experts design the security. But that's not the point. I feel pretty certain I can guess what Emma has been telling you. Am I right?'

Gently shrugged. 'She gave me certain information.'

'Yes. Touching Leslie Phipps. I did hope the girl would be more discreet.'

'The information was pertinent.'

'Of course, of course! But perhaps you should allow for a degree of bias. I don't need to tell you that the girl feels guilty, and your going after Timothy touches a nerve. She didn't treat Timothy very well, so now she feels herself responsible for him. I think it likely she may have overplayed her hand, and given you some exaggerated ideas.'

'There is no truth in what she was telling me?'

'I didn't say that, either! To be quite frank, I greatly favoured the idea of my own son having a hand in the book.'

'To his taking it over?'

'No – now we come to it. I dropped that project very quickly. I did hint at it to Phipps, that he could expect a fair sum if he agreed to turn the book over, but quite apart from his negative reaction, I soon saw how damaging it would be to lose him. Phipps is an authority, a leading authority, there can be no question about that. We needed to have his name on the cover. But that seemed no reason why Laurence's shouldn't be there too.'

'To which Phipps was more agreeable?'

'Well, I have to be frank with you. Phipps dug his heels in all the way. But it was surely a reasonable favour to ask, that a member of the family should have a part in it.'

'So you continued to press him?'

'Not precisely that! Let's say I left the deal on the table.'

'Perhaps – raising the ante?'

Sir Charles gave Gently a look that was less than friendly. 'Anyway,' he said. 'I felt it was best to give you the plain facts of the matter. I think you may agree that it doesn't require a great deal of serious consideration.'

Gently said: 'Yet it does have a bearing.'

'Only, I submit, in the mind of Miss Emma.'

Gently said: 'Yet it might have been helpful to have had this information from the first.'

Sir Charles stared at the Constable. 'Ye-es, very well, then,' he said. 'I accept that.'

'With', Gently said, 'any other pertinent information that has yet to come to hand.'

'Oh, damnation!' Sir Charles exclaimed. 'Do you think I'm holding out on you, George? But I take your point. I understand. I should have told you about Phipps myself. I didn't, because it was painful, because perhaps it made me

66

look like an old fool. But that's all. I'm not hiding information. Whoever shot my son, I want to see punished.'

Gently said nothing. Sir Charles glowered at the Constable. It was a painting that Gently didn't remember having seen reproduced: a farmhouse, behind trees and a pond, with a woman and a child feeding ducks in the foreground, and behind the farmhouse a sunlit harvest-field dotted with golden sheaves of wheat. It wasn't a huge canvas, but it was arresting in its moment of vision, its luminous colour. Sir Charles kept his gaze on it. He said:

'You'd be right. You'd be right if you took me for an old fool. I loved my son. I wanted him here. But I set everyone against him. He was my son by another marriage, a stranger come from overseas, and I made too much of him, Mary's boy, the son my first wife never lived to see. I can't blame them, really, Daphne, Timothy, Cassandra. Hugh. Leslie Phipps. I rubbed their noses in him too often. But hate him . . . as much as this? I can't believe that. I can't. Either it was some sort of devilish accident, or you had better start looking somewhere else.' He paused. 'And would that be so impossible?'

Gently still said nothing.

'What I mean is,' Sir Charles said, 'we know very little of his background in Australia. He had parted from his wife, we know that, and he had a house in a suburb of Sydney. But he never said much about his life there, or indeed why he came home at all.'

Gently said: 'You are suggesting that an enemy followed him here?'

'Surely stranger things have been known.'

'One who knew the way into the gun-room?'

Sir Charles turned to stare at him. Then away. He said: 'The trouble is, nothing else makes sense. I can't believe it of Hugh or anyone else. To loathe is one thing, to murder quite another. If it wasn't an accident . . . then who?'

Down the hall, through the glass doors, one could see the tea-party breaking up; Cassandra going up the stairs with her mother, Brewster departing to another part of the house. Then came Emma Spinks. She stared towards the gallery, before running up the stairs after the two other women. And finally Phipps, who also stared at the gallery. But turned away. And went out down the steps.

5

Gently excused himself, and left Sir Charles switching out the lights. Phipps hadn't gone far. At the bottom of the lawn stood a garden seat, beside a statue; and there the writer had seated himself, and was filling and lighting a pipe. He observed Gently's approach with a cynical stare, but went on with what he was doing. Gently seated himself beside him. He also produced and filled his pipe. Up at the house, for a brief moment, the figure of Sir Charles appeared in the porch, then vanished again. Phipps tilted his head to exhale smoke. He said:

'What shall we discuss – shall it be literature, art, or the state of the nation?'

Gently pressed his match into the turf. 'Perhaps your vigil on Sunday would be more germane.'

'My vigil, indeed! But that's too dull. It involved merely the perusal of the so-called "qualities". In passing, I expect you may have noticed how decadent the Sunday papers have become.'

'Between lunch and tea.'

'Yes, how I wasted my time! So much paper and ink and triviality. I believe I drowsed for part of the time. It was probably between *The Times* and the *Telegraph*.'

'And that's all you have to tell me?'

'Just filling in the gaps. Between distant thuds and passing Aussies. Is there more you require?'

'Suppose I were to tell you that I have testimony that you weren't in the garden.'

Phipps delicately exhaled smoke. 'Then you are dealing with a liar. Provided your informer was less than fictitious.'

'If they passed through the garden, and didn't see you?'

'I suppose defective eyesight is not impossible.'

'You continue to assert that you spent the afternoon there?'

'Entirely, absolutely and with incredible unction.'

'I see.'

Phipps eyed a passing cloud. 'And may we move on, now, to art? With possibly literature as a second string, since both are stirring in the air here?'

'You wish to discuss that?'

'Oh, not particularly. But I am certifiably not an idiot. You are fresh from a session with our little lady, and after that with a solemn Sir Charles. Let me add to your probable information. I was offered a cool twenty thousand. I turned it down. I was offered double. Such is the price of professional integrity.'

He drew on his pipe with a jerk, and punched smoke into the evening air.

'But – you were not to be bought.'

Phipps eyed him waspishly. 'Have you sampled the products of the late deceased? They comprise an admixture of the three S's, namely Sex, Sadism and Snobbery, conveyed in a prose so redundant that one should be paid to wade through it. What Sir Charles was suggesting, we will allow in ignorance, was my consent to professional suicide. And in answer to your asseveration, no: not if the price had been doubly redoubled.'

Gently wafted smoke. 'Yet the project was not permitted to die.'

'As far as it concerned me, it had never climbed out of its grave.'

'You would be under pressure.'

'I can live with pressure.'

'Sir Charles was desperate to keep his son with him.'

'He had my answer.'

'But the pressure was there. A pressure which since has been relieved.'

'By me, you are asserting?' Phipps's eyes were scathing.

'By someone with similar qualifications. Yours include being the last-known person to see him alive, and probably testing positive for use of a gun.'

'That – and nothing else?'

'That, and a query against your statement.'

'Then I must withhold my congratulations, musn't I? Because your job here still remains to be done.' He eased back in the seat, took quick puffs, then pointed with his pipe towards the house. 'Regard that domicile in che- quered flint, lit now so appealingly by evening sun! Apart from the housekeeper and maid, about whose leisure hours I know little, name me one inmate, just one, who wouldn't test positive for use of a gun. Guns are the staple at Warren Lodge. I had one in my hand the day I arrived here. Sir Charles shoots, his children shoot, Lady Daphne even has a saddle-holster. If the present situation hadn't made it bad taste, you would probably have had a gun pressed on you by now. You may say it is regrettable, but thus it is. One qualification goes out of the window.'

'One qualification.'

Phipps struck a fresh light. His hand was steady and deliberate. 'And the others? A degree of motive, and a sight of the victim rushing to his doom.'

'And one more.'

'I was forgetting. Your informant with the defective eyes. Well, I concede. There was an interval when my presence in the garden was not available.'

Gently said nothing.

'A call of nature,' Phipps said. 'Followed by a thirst for

something cool. And before you ask me, I met no one. The. house just then appeared to be deserted.'

'You went up to the house?'

'To the offices first. Then to the lounge-bar for a beer.'

'Meeting no one.'

'I have to confess it.'

'At what time was this?'

'Getting on for four.'

Gently gave Phipps a long look: Phipps returned it with unflinching gaze. He looked away.

'Drawn match, would you say? Or should I submit to the handcuffs now?'

But just then there was a crunching of gravel, and Calthorpe's Escort appeared in the drive. He got out, and was about to head for the house when he caught sight of Gently on the lawn. Gently rose and went to him. Calthorpe came trotting down the terrace steps.

'Sir – that witness we were needing! Well, he's just walked into the police station. And he's got the goods. We can nail Merton. We could have this case sewn up tonight.'

'He just . . . walked in?'

'Yes, sir. And after all the chasing about we've done! He's a bloke who works at the wood-yard, and he was taking a walk in the forest on Sunday.'

'He was taking a walk.'

'Yes, sir.'

'And he saw what happened?'

'Not exactly that, sir! But what he did see was Merton, and Merton had a gun, and he was a lot closer to the dell than he's letting on. Gourbold, that's the bloke's name, sir, was crossing the main ride, coming back from the brecks. He knows Merton, who's often at the yard, and he saw him up the ride, heading towards the dell. Well, Gourbold goes on his way, and after a while he hears the shot, but he's not to know, he thinks it's Merton having a bang at the rabbits or something. Then, at work today, there's this gossip about us having Merton at the station, so he decides he'd better have a word. And when he knocks off, he comes in.'

'Is he giving us a time?'

'Says a bit after three, sir.'

'And he's sure about the gun?'

'That's what he says. I thought you'd want to see him yourself, sir, and I made him wait while I went to fetch you.'

'So let's go!'

Ten minutes later the Escort was reparked outside the police station, and Gently being introduced to a grubby-looking youngster clad in jeans and a soiled sports-shirt. He had jumped up apprehensively when they entered.

'I should be getting back – they'll be wondering . . .!'

'Sit down, Gourbold.'

'Yes, but I'm late! I should be home now, having my tea.'

'Just take a seat.'

'Yes, but . . .'

'We'll try to keep this as brief as we can.'

Reluctantly, Gourbold resumed his chair. There was sweat on his smirched face. He had tousled hair much in need of a comb, and his eyes flickered nervously at Gently as the latter took his seat behind the desk.

'I ought really . . .'

Gently just stared at him. 'Now. I think you have something to tell us.'

'But I've told this man already – '

'I would like you to go through it again with me.'

'But I just saw Mr Merton – '

'From the beginning. What were you doing out there on Sunday?'

Gourbold was sweating more than ever. But he couldn't keep his eyes from Gently's. He made a manner of appealing gesture towards him.

73

'Look, I wasn't up to anything, honest! I just went to have a look at the old tank. If there's anything missing, it wasn't me.'

'You went to look at the tank.'

'Yes. I mean, there can't be much left – '

'At what time was that?'

'Time? It was after lunch, I don't know – '

'Between two and three?'

'Yes, I reckon.'

'Who else did you see out there?'

'No one! I was on my own. But that doesn't mean to say – '

'For example, did you meet any horse-riders?'

'Oh, that! Yes, I did see one of those. But not near the tank, it wasn't. They were miles away, across the other side.'

'They?'

'Well, him. I don't know.'

'It was a man?'

'I tell you, I don't know! It was miles away, over by the forest.'

'Go on,' Gently said.

Gourbold swept damp hair from his face. 'Well, I had a look round the old tank, didn't I, but there wasn't anything worth having, so after a bit I came away again.'

'You came through the forest?'

'Well, yes, it's shortest. We live in those cottages on the road to Sweffley.'

'Which took you across the main ride.'

'Yes. That's where you cut through.'

'And?'

Gourbold dabbed some more. 'So I saw him there, didn't I? Mr Merton. I knew who it was. He's around all the time, telling them where to fell and when to fetch in the timber. So there he was, going up the ride. Gun and all. I saw him.'

'You saw him, but he didn't see you?'

74

'No! He was away up the ride, wasn't he?'

'But close enough for you to see he was carrying a gun?'

'Yes. I could see it. He'd got a gun.'

'And he was carrying it, how?'

'Like . . . I don't know!'

'You could see the gun, but not how he carried it?'

'Well . . . like under his arm, I reckon!' Still Gourbold couldn't drag his eyes away from Gently's.

Gently said: 'Under his arm. As one might, for example, carry a stick. Was it like that?'

'Yes, like that. Under his arm. Like it was a stick.'

'But it was a gun, and not a stick?'

'I'm telling you, it was a gun!'

'And you were how far away from him?'

'He was up the ride – I don't know!'

'You don't know.' Gently pondered a moment on the grimy, sweating face. 'I think you should understand, Gourbold, that we shall require a written statement, signed and countersigned, to be used in evidence. Into that statement you will be well advised to put nothing except what you are certain of.' Gourbold goggled at him. 'Well?'

'I don't know – he'd got something!'

'Something?'

'That's how it looked, like he'd got something under his arm.'

'And that something was a gun?'

'Well, I heard a shot, didn't I?'

'In your statement, will you say it was a gun?'

At last Gourbold dragged his eyes away.

Gently said: 'Did you see Merton at all?'

'Yes, I did! And it's the truth I'm telling you.'

'So where did you see him?'

'Up the ride, like I said. He was going up the ride, near the top.'

'How long after that did you hear the shot?'

'Ten minutes, could have been quarter of an hour. I was

75

nearly through to the road. Then I heard him pop off back there.'

Gently said: 'You are telling us this now. Why didn't you give your information sooner?'

'Because – because I knew it was going to be like this!'

Gently said: 'Just that?'

Gourbold did his best to face him. He failed.

'The young devil!' Calthorpe exploded, after Bodney had led Gourbold away to write his statement. 'He was having us on. He never saw any gun, and ten to one he never saw Merton either!'

'A put-up job . . .?'

'Of course it was.' Even Calthorpe's moustache seemed to bristle. 'He's got it in for Merton, that's what, probably something that happened at work. I can just see it – Merton caught him at something – pinching some gear, it wouldn't surprise me. Either that, or he's been looting that tank, and thinks we're going to hear about it.'

Gently shrugged. 'It could be like that.'

'I know his type, sir. But don't you worry. I'll have Bodney turn his pad over, and if there's any gear there his feet won't touch.'

Gently grinned at the local man. 'Any petty misdemeanours you're welcome to! In the mean while, do we know at what time they knock off at the wood-yard?'

'When they knock off, sir?'

'When they knock off.'

'Well . . . as far as I know, at five, sir.'

'At about the time you were turning Timothy Stanton loose?'

Calthorpe stared at him in a wild surmise. 'You think . . . Gourbold was got at, sir?'

Gently said: 'At least, the coincidence is suggestive.'

'Yes, sir – yes!' Calthorpe's eyes were sharp. 'And it was

hard on five when he left here. We offered him transport, but he turned it down. So he'd have run into that lot just leaving off.'

'You offered him transport?'

'Yes, sir. And he told us what we could do with it.'

'So he may have been planning to catch Gourbold.'

'Has to be that, sir. And right after we'd given him a positive test.'

'Interesting,' Gently said. 'Though we might have difficulty in actually proving it.'

'But Gourbold was lying his head off, sir! And there could only be one person who put him up to it. So like that Timothy Stanton has got questions to answer – it could be he's in this up to his neck.'

'You think Gourbold was lying at all points?'

'About the gun, sir. He was lying about that.'

'But about the rest?'

'I can't think why not, sir.'

Gently stared for a moment over Calthorpe's head. He said: 'For the most part, I was ready to believe him. I think he may well have gone scrounging where he says, and then taken a route home through the forest. And so he may have seen Merton, if not the gun. He may have seen Merton heading up the ride. And I'm prepared to accept that he heard the shot ten or fifteen minutes after seeing Merton.'

Calthorpe hesitated. 'You could just be right, sir.'

Gently said: 'None of which favours Merton.'

After another pause, Calthorpe said: 'Shall we have him in, sir?'

Gently nodded; and felt for his pipe.

There was less buck about Merton this time. He entered and took his place almost meekly. He sat a little bowed, his blue eyes wary, his freckled hands creeping together on his knees. Just for an instant he had glanced at the window, at

77

the parked cars, the passers-by outside; then his mouth had set bleakly and he'd returned his stare to the desk. Calthorpe closed the office door and took his seat. Gently laid down his pipe. He said:

'We have been pursuing our investigation, Merton, and certain fresh facts have come to our attention. But before we go into that, would you care to enlarge on the statement you gave us?'

Merton gave him a quick baffled look. 'Just what are you trying to get me to say now?'

Gently said: 'I'm giving you an opportunity. By now, you'll have had time to think things over.'

Merton's mouth twisted. 'Oh no! I'm not going to fall for a trick like that. All I'm saying I've said already, so stop wasting my time and yours.'

Gently said: 'Then we'll come to the facts. We have spoken to Robinson, your ranger. He agrees that he reported the trouble in section 10, but says the report was made a fortnight ago.'

Merton's gaze jumped at him. 'So what are you saying?'

'I'm saying that the matter was scarcely urgent. Yet you are asking me to believe that you would devote a Sunday afternoon to it.'

'But I did!'

'You still say so?'

'Oh lord, can't I make you understand?' Merton exclaimed. 'It was just because it was a fortnight since that it was time for another look. Robinson found the eggs. Eggs take time to hatch. Until they do, it isn't time to spray. So yes, it was absolutely the right time for an inspection of section 10.'

'But . . . on a Sunday afternoon?'

'Why not on a Sunday afternoon? Cassandra had gone riding, I don't watch football, and I'm not a bosom pal of Timothy's.'

Gently shook his head. 'You must expect to have it questioned.'

'Then question away. I don't care.'

Gently said: 'Especially in the light of testimony that places you at some distance from section 10.'

'Testimony?'

Gently said nothing.

'But there was no one around to give any testimony! I met nobody, going or coming, so how could anyone give you testimony?'

Gently said: 'An employee at the wood-yard had been across to the old tank. He was returning through the forest when he caught sight of you in the main ride.'

'An employee?'

'One who knows you.'

Merton's stare was hard. 'And I can guess who that is! A lout I've had to speak to a few times. He won't be doing me any favours, and you'd be a fool to take his word for anything.' He paused. 'So what's he saying?'

'That he saw you in the ride.'

'But I've admitted that!'

'At the further end.'

'At – ?'

'A short while before he heard the report of the gun. In addition, he formed the impression that you were carrying something, it may have been a stick, under your arm.'

'A – stick?'

'In the first instance, he referred to it as a gun.'

The freckled face was aghast. 'And you – you're going to believe him?'

Gently said: 'Were you carrying something?'

'No, I wasn't. I damn well wasn't!'

'Not a stick?'

'Nor a gun. Nor any damn thing at all. The fellow's lying, can't you see that? He's made up a tale to land me in it.'

79

Gently said: 'Yet a gun was used there. And not very long after witness claims to have seen you.'

'But he was lying. I didn't take my gun. For all I knew, it was still in the gun-room.'

'Because it was a Sunday, you wouldn't have taken it?'

'Because it was a Sunday. Yes. Yes.'

'You would have been so particular?'

'Oh God!' Merton groaned. 'You're going to stick me with that gun, aren't you?'

Gently said: 'Accidents happen. And that gun was certainly taken there. And your brother-in-law died because of it. Might we not suppose a simple explanation?'

'Only it wasn't like that!'

'It wasn't?'

'No – I mean, it wasn't to do with me! I was just there, going about my business, and no bloody guns stuck under my arm either.'

'You simply went to the section to conduct a check.'

'Yes. I simply went to the section.'

'By the way you described to us.'

'By the way . . .' Merton hesitated. 'What did that lying hound Gourbold tell you?'

Gently said: 'We have inspected that route. It involves an unusual degree of obstruction. You presumably are familiar with the forest. I would have expected you to choose a different way.'

Merton looked sullen. 'So you're going to believe Gourbold?'

Gently said: 'As far as common sense supports him.'

Merton looked away. 'All damn right, then! Perhaps I did use the way from the top of the ride.'

'So why did you lie to us?'

'Why? When it passes right by the spot where the Aussie was killed? Of course I wasn't going to let on about that – didn't you have enough with me just being there?'

'You didn't hesitate to lie?'

'So I was a fool. But that doesn't make me a murderer, either.'

'And you passed that spot going and coming?'

Merton's chin stuck out. 'I passed that spot.'

Gently said: 'And?'

Merton stared at the desk. 'And I didn't see anything, going or coming. It must have happened while I was at the section. Then the fellow had cleared off before I got back there.'

'You hadn't heard the shot?'

Through his teeth, Merton said: 'Perhaps I lied about that too.'

'You heard the shot, and you passed the spot where your brother-in-law lay bleeding to death?'

'You bastard,' Merton said. 'I wasn't to know that.'

'Laurence Stanton could still be living today.'

'I didn't know that!' His mouth was quivering. 'Do you think I wouldn't have helped him, if I'd known he was there?'

'You didn't see him. You didn't see anything.'

'How many more times? No!'

'And I may depend on that for the truth?'

Merton stared at him bitterly, helplessly.

'Very well.' Gently reached for his pipe. 'We seem to have made a degree of progress. You did take the route that passes the dell, and you now admit to hearing the shot. Have you anything to add?'

'Go to hell!'

'We shall, of course, require you to revise your statement.'

'And then – do I get out of here?'

Gently lit his pipe. He didn't seem to hear.

When Calthorpe returned to the office he had a sheet of statement-paper in his hand. The statement on it was brief

81

and in scrupulous policese, though written in a scrawling, uneducated hand. Calthorpe laid it before Gently.

'Not even a stick, sir! He just sees Merton going up the ride. Do you think we could have been too hasty, sir, in frightening him off a mention of the gun?'

Gently blew smoke over the statement. 'Can you see him standing up to cross-questioning?'

'Well – no, sir! But this is what I've been thinking while you were turning over chummie here.' Calthorpe took a seat opposite Gently. 'It's like this. We think young Stanton put Gourbold up to it. Well, so he might have. But just suppose he knows something he doesn't want to come out with. I mean, it could put him in wrong with the family if he was to tip us off about Merton, but this way he can do it and nobody any the wiser.'

'You mean – about the gun?'

'Especially the gun, sir. Though it could have been about spotting Merton as well. And young Stanton was on the loose all that afternoon. No reason why he shouldn't have seen what was going on.'

Gently blew more smoke at the statement. 'But then, why would he want to give us Merton?'

'Well, anything, sir. Maybe there's a grudge. We're not to know what goes on in the family.'

'Merton is his brother-in-law.'

'It needn't cut any ice. And we were having a go at Master Timothy. But what I'm saying is that perhaps this Gourbold is a gift-horse, and we shouldn't be looking him in the mouth.'

Gently brooded over his pipe. 'On the other hand, we know now that he does have it in for Merton.'

'So that would make him just the tool for young Stanton, sir. All he would need to do was brief him about the gun.'

'About the gun, he would need no briefing.'

'But it's on the cards, sir. It could have happened that

way. And then we could be sure that Merton did have the gun, like we've got a witness at second hand.'

'Or a liar at second hand?'

'Well . . . there's that, sir!'

Gently shrugged, and flicked the statement. 'What we have got now is the certainty that Merton was close to the dell at least twice and a strong suspicion that Timothy Stanton is in this deeper than he cares to admit. Any advance on that?'

Sadly, Calthorpe shook his head.

'So on that basis we will proceed. I will pursue it at the Lodge, while you go on combing the area for witnesses.'

'And Merton, sir?'

'Stays where he is. To concentrate his own mind and other people's.' Gently rose and knocked out his pipe. 'Just keep him well fed,' he said.

6

Gently rang Gabrielle, then they got back into Calthorpe's car. Breckford's drooping main street looked quieter than ever at this hour of the long summer evening. Shops, businesses were firmly closed; scarcely a vehicle was parked down the whole length of the street. A dog-walker and a hard-breathing jogger were the only pedestrians in view. Across the river, the lengthening sun lit up the machinery of the deserted wood-yard, and revealed a touch of pink in the ranked stems of distant pines.

'Where do you recommend I put up?'

'The Cross Keys, sir. It's all there is.'

And here there were signs of life, in the low-ceilinged bar, the adjacent lounge. Gently booked in and ordered pints. The publican himself came to deal with them. A comfortable-looking man in his fifties, he eyed the two policemen with curiosity. With a nod of his head, he said:

'It's a rum old business, up there!'

Gently took a long pull before replying: 'Did you ever see that fellow in here?'

'You mean the Aussie? Blast yes. His old man brought him in, didn't he?'

'Sir Charles?'

'Right you are. And got him drinking pints of bitter.'

'Was that unusual?'

'It was for him, squire. All he wanted was Foster's lager.

84

But Sir Charles told him it was kid's stuff, that what he needed was Norwich bitter.'

'And the Aussie accepted that?'

'Oh, ah. He made a face, but he gót it down him. But he was in here a few times after that, and it was always Foster's lager then.'

'He came in with other people?'

'Once or twice. Once with that mawther who works up there.'

'Anyone else?'

'Ah. Mr Timothy. But I doubt if they got on any too well.'

Gently drank. 'Mr Timothy.'

'Well, yes, he's often in here,' the publican said. 'We see the others once in a blue moon, but Mr Timothy is a regular.' He turned and pointed behind him. On the wall, among posters, hung a framed painting of The Cross Keys. 'I was fool enough to buy that off him, but don't go asking me what I paid for it.'

'That's one of his?'

'Right.' The publican considered it fondly. Though possibly not dripping with talent, it showed more acquaintance with the pictures in the gallery than with those displayed on the houseboat. 'All right, then. Ask me.'

'I'm asking,' Gently said.

'A hundred quid,' the publican said. 'Now you tell me whether I've been had.'

Gently drank, but didn't tell him. 'So Timothy Stanton is a regular,' he said.

'Pretty regular,' the publican said. 'I dare say I've had my hundred quid back.'

'He has friends here?'

'Dunno about friends. But he isn't stand-offish, I'll give him that.'

'He'll have a word with people.'

'Ah.'

'Like that group down the bar.'

'Ah. With them.'

The publican turned his head to look. The group, comprised of three youths, were engaged with the dart-board. Dressed in soiled jeans, soiled shirts and soiled trainers, they clearly belonged to the Gourbold stable.

'Thirsty work in the yard,' the publican said.

'Would you know a youngster called Gourbold?' Gently said.

'He's a mate of theirs,' the publican said. 'But here I stand gassing. Do you gents want a refill?'

In the car, Calthorpe said: 'Not a lot of doubt now, sir.' Then he added, in a tone of restrained admiration: 'Do you think he had him, over that painting?'

Gently had Calthorpe drop him at the Lodge gates, and from the drive took the path to the moorings. Down the path, the warm air was scented by the honeysuckle that climbed luxuriantly over trees and undergrowth. Then, as he emerged from the trees, he became aware of music and of an admirable tenor voice: on this occasion, at all events, Timothy Stanton was relaxing with Britten and Pearsy. Gently found him reclining in the well. He stepped aboard. Timothy Stanton waved a hand.

'Do take a seat. This will soon be over.'

Gently reached across and switched off the tape-player.

'Oh, you naughty man!' Timothy Stanton pouted. 'Don't they teach you any manners in the police force?'

Now Gently took a seat. He said: 'I've been talking to a friend of yours. Gourbold. He mentioned a gun. Then it became a stick. Then it vanished from his account altogether.'

'How vexing for you,' Timothy Stanton said. 'I've had the same thing happen to me. And with guns being so important for you. I trust you gave him a piece of your mind.'

Gently said: 'When did you last see Gourbold?'

'Let me see,' Timothy Stanton said. 'Do you know, I can't really remember. As a peasant, he fails to be memorable. I may have played darts with him, last Friday week.'

'I think it was today.'

'Oh, never!'

'When he left his place of work. At five p.m.'

'Surely not!'

'And if he should say any different?'

'Then he's a liar,' Timothy Stanton said. 'But I thought you knew that.'

Gently regarded the evening stream. 'Perhaps we should do some adding up,' he said. 'When someone takes such risks to throw blame on another, it can often be an interesting exercise. Let us suppose your brother-in-law is innocent. Who does that leave with the strongest motive? With opportunity? With access to the weapon? With evidence of having recently used such a weapon? And if we can add to that, tampering with a witness to bear testimony to another's prejudice?'

Timothy Stanton was no longer lounging. He said: 'Oh no – oh no! Because you'd have to prove that.'

'That you bribed Gourbold?'

'That – and the rest. But with Gourbold, it would be his word against mine.'

'Because there were no witnesses?'

'Because! It's you who are saying all this, not me. And you can go on saying it as long as you like. I don't see why it should bother me.'

Gently said: 'We might act on our suspicions.'

'Lawyers, money and influence,' Timothy Stanton said. 'That's what you'll be up against. I'm not your dear Hugh. For a Stanton, we mortgage the family silver.'

To the river, Gently said: 'I wouldn't put my faith in it.'

'Oh, I think it's worth a try,' Timothy Stanton said.

'A plea of irresistible impulse might serve you better.'

'So sweet of you', Timothy Stanton said, 'to advise me.'

Gently went on admiring the river. 'I think your sister knows something,' he said. 'Of course, your sister is torn two ways, and it might come to her choosing between a husband and a brother. Which will it be?'

From the corner of his eye, he saw Timothy Stanton tense. After a moment, he said:

'How clever we're getting. Only Cassie was out riding, and miles away.'

'Not miles away,' Gently said. 'Surely she's told you?'

'Yes, she has. She was nowhere near there.'

'She wasn't riding the horse. The one that came by the dell. That paused for a while, by the boundary fence?'

'There wasn't such a horse!'

Gently nodded. 'A horse that was reined in, and stood for a time. As though the rider had seen something of interest. Either in the dell, or in the ride approaching it.' Gently shrugged. 'Of course, it could have been your mother, or some other person entirely. If the latter, we will find him. But there was certainly a witness at the dell.'

'I don't believe this – you're just being clever!'

'If it was your sister, she has to make that choice.'

'But what choice? I was never out there. I was here, right here, where I'm sitting now!'

'Yet . . . something she would have seen?'

Timothy Stanton was staring. Suddenly, pettishly, he switched on the tape-player. Without bothering to turn his head, Gently reached across and switched it off again. He said:

'What Gourbold told us, and then went back on, was that he saw a gun in a certain person's possession. We think he was primed to tell us that. But he may not have been primed with a lie.'

'And you think – ?'

Gently said to the river: 'There could have been another

witness. That follows. One who had opportunity to be in the forest, and with possibly a motive for going there.'

For a long moment, Timothy Stanton hung on; then his head began to shake with increasing vigour. 'Oh no! You're out to get me. And I'm not going to fall into a trap like that.'

'You think it's a trap?'

'I know it's a trap! You want me to say I was in the forest. Then the next thing, it's me with the gun. Oh no. I was here. Now you prove different.'

'Then Gourbold was primed with a malicious lie?'

'If you like. But not by me.'

'If not by you, then by whom?'

Timothy Stanton switched on the tape-player. Gently switched it off again.

Gently said: 'Let's go back to that Sunday afternoon. Your girl-friend has been stolen and you've been given a hiding. You see your stepbrother make off towards the forest. And the door of the tack-room is conveniently left open. Can we regard it as a credible moment for you to settle down to a programme of music?'

Timothy Stanton jerked away from him. 'I do so love sarcasm,' he said. 'You should stay on here. It would cheer the scene up. With us, sarcasm is almost a lost art.'

'A credible moment?'

Timothy Stanton said nothing.

'The house, the grounds, virtually deserted,' Gently said. 'Your mother and sister out on their horses, your father engrossed with television, Mr Brewster settled in the library, Mr Phipps secure in the Round Garden. By now, your brother-in-law would have departed for his visit to section 10, Miss Spinks was out with the dogs, the other two staff retired to their quarters. Not a soul about to see you. Not a soul in the stable-yard. All that was to be done, could be done. Though it might have been wiser to have left a tape playing.'

'But, I tell you – !'

Gently shook his head. 'A witness who should have heard music, didn't.'

'But nobody came here ... there couldn't have been a witness!'

'A witness who should have heard music. But didn't.'

Timothy Stanton pulled round to stare at Gently. Gently had only time for the river.

'But I could have been changing tapes,' Timothy Stanton said. 'Look, I mean, one doesn't always play them one after another! I probably wasn't, in fact I remember. Once or twice I gave myself an interval.'

'You were unlucky,' Gently said. 'That witness could have sworn that you never left the houseboat.'

'But I didn't!'

'On the strength of some music. If only you had thought to leave some playing.'

'But – !'

'No music,' Gently said. 'But of course, I am not contending that this was planned. Circumstances are against it. You were in a state of high emotion. All that was uppermost in your mind would be revenge.'

'But this is completely and utterly fabulous!'

'You had the motive that counts,' Gently said. 'Beside it, your brother-in-law's is venal. What happened in the forest was an act of revenge.'

'No, it wasn't!'

'It wasn't ... ?'

'It didn't have to be at all. Hugh was counting on that cottage, and he wasn't the only one with a motive.'

'You know of others?'

'Yes – Phippsy! I dare say they haven't told you about him.'

'They've told me about him.'

'So why not him?'

Slowly, Gently shook his head at the river.

'Oh no,' Timothy Stanton said bitingly. 'It couldn't be Phippsy, could it? Phippsy has his bourgeois reputation behind him, while I'm just the family failure. Isn't that how it goes?'

Gently shrugged.

'Yes, that's how it goes,' Timothy Stanton said. 'I'm the black sheep, and I don't have an alibi. So when the chips are down, who else could it be?' He stared very hard at Gently. 'You don't believe me, do you?' he said. 'Whatever I tell you is just a lie. Even if it's the truth, you still won't believe me.'

Gently didn't even shrug.

'So listen to this,' Timothy Stanton said. 'I may as well have my say. Believe it or not, but I do have an alibi, and it's what you were asking me about on the phone.'

'You mean ... the containers?'

'Yes, the bloody containers! I know I lied about it on the phone. But that was because you were trying to use it to place me in the stable-yard. Well, I did go up for some water, but I didn't go to the stable-yard. I used the tap by the greenhouse, which is the other end from the stable-yard.'

'Passing', Gently said, 'by the library window.'

'Yes,' Timothy Stanton said. 'Yes. Passing by the library window. Where Dennys saw me. Just the way he told you.'

'At ... around three thirty?'

Timothy Stanton gazed at him. 'You sneering devil!' he said. 'So you don't believe me. Even though it's true. And just because it doesn't suit your book. Well, it's on the table, that's what happened, and that's when the music wasn't playing.'

'On the table,' Gently said.

Timothy Stanton jerked his gaze away.

91

Then there were footsteps on the bank, and Brewster came doubtfully up to the houseboat. He smiled, guiltily.

'Don't let me interrupt! But I come with a mission from on high. Sir Charles asked me to tell you, if I ran across you, that you're invited to join us at dinner.'

'Dennys!' Timothy Stanton burst out. 'Dennys – tell him, Dennys! Tell him it's true, and that you did see me, going past to fill my containers!'

Dennys Brewster looked more embarrassed than ever. He smiled at Timothy Stanton, smiled at Gently. He said:

'Oh dear! The trouble is I don't think our friend here is going to believe me.'

'But you must tell him – he wants to arrest me!'

'Dear me, we can't have that!' Brewster grinned. 'Especially right on top of dinner. But I'm sure our friend isn't being serious. You're not the one he's after, are you?'

'You know I'm not – how could I be?'

'Well, I know you can't be,' Brewster said. 'But me, I'm in a privileged position, which our friend isn't able to share.' He glanced appealingly at Gently. 'You aren't about to arrest Timothy, are you?' he said. 'Because if you are, you'll have to take me in too, for trying to pervert the ends of justice. Not', he added hastily, 'that I'm admitting that! But I could see your point of view.'

Gently said: 'You maintain that you saw Stanton?'

'Only if you believe me,' Brewster said. 'And I don't think it would hurt you, or not very much. Young Timothy is such an unlikely prospect.'

'Thank you for nothing,' Timothy Stanton said. 'I've just been sketched in as a hate-crazed killer.'

'Hush, you're too sensitive!' Brewster said. 'It's your artistic nature coming out, my son. Did you admit to it?'

'Take a running jump!'

'Ah, these painters!' Brewster said to Gently. 'I assume

you have been trying him for size, and that's the reason for his present excitement.'

Gently turned again to the river. He said: 'After lunch, how long did you spend in the library?'

'Oh dear, it's my turn,' Brewster said. 'And personally, I don't have a leg to stand on.'

'So how long?'

'Till four or after. Perhaps Sir Charles can tell you when. I saw only the second half of the match, and probably only half an hour of that.'

Gently said: 'You realize that doesn't cover you.'

'Alas, only too vividly,' Brewster said. 'I should have waved to Timothy when he went by, and you should be plaguing him to give me an alibi.'

'In fact, you don't have one.'

'Not a whisper. I had opportunity in handfuls. Motive I'm rather short on, but perhaps I didn't like the cut of his jib. Otherwise, I'm almost indecently qualified. You could run me in without a second thought.'

'You stayed in the library.'

'That's my story.'

'And saw Timothy Stanton pass by.'

'Now you're asking me to stick my neck out!' Brewster said. 'Dare I say yes, and hope to get away with it? Well, I did. I saw our Timothy. He had a four-gallon container in either hand. And before you ask me, it was around three, and he was heading for the tap used by the gardener.'

Gently said: 'Very circumstantial.'

'He still doesn't believe me,' Brewster sighed. 'I'm probably just sticking up for the son of the house, and hoping for a handshake on top of my fee.'

Timothy Stanton said: 'I'm fed up with all this. You saw me up there, and that's an end to it. I didn't do it, and I'm certain you didn't, so now he can get back to chasing Hugh.'

'Hush, hush!' Brewster said. 'He isn't such a bad sort,

either. But you make a point. And I'm sure he takes it. And that's all we should expect before dinner.'

'I'm going,' Timothy Stanton said. 'If his highness permits it.'

'Do you?' Brewster smiled, at Gently's back.

'For the present,' Gently told the river.

'I hope you sit there and get rheumatism,' Timothy Stanton said.

Nevertheless there was some hesitation before Timothy Stanton left the houseboat, as though perhaps he felt his pride involved in leaving Gently in possession. But Gently sat on immovable, and finally Timothy Stanton jumped on to the bank. Gently heard Brewster addressing soothing words to him, then the sound of their footsteps departing up the bank. He sat silent a while longer, watching the first tendrils of mist climb over the still water, breathing in the odour of meadowsweet, listening to a sedge-warbler in the reeds. Then, without turning his head, he said:

'It's all right. You can come out now.'

There was a gasp from the interior of the houseboat. A curtain rustled, there was a faint scuffle, and Cassandra Merton emerged to confront Gently.

'You beast. You knew I was there all the time!'

'Do take a seat, Mrs Merton.'

'But how? How did you know?'

Gently pointed to a strut at the end of the well. From it hung Timothy Stanton's shaving-mirror.

'Oh!' Cassandra Merton stormed. 'That's sneaky. I'm glad now I did what I did. I saw you going off towards the moorings, and I decided to stalk you down here. I suppose you saw me slip aboard, and everything?'

Gently nodded.

'Then all that joshing of Timothy – it was for my benefit?'

'Not entirely.'

94

'But you knew I was there! You were making jolly certain I should get a good earful.' Her brown eyes riveted on his. 'Just tell me this. Is it true that my brother has bribed a witness – that someone is telling you they saw Hugh in the forest, and that Hugh was carrying his gun?'

'Sit down, Mrs Merton.'

'Just tell me!'

'Such a statement has been made to us.'

'And Timothy is behind it?'

'That is a possibility.'

'Oh, my God. My own brother.'

Now she did sit, taking the chair that Timothy Stanton had vacated. Her eyes dwelt on Gently's a little longer, then swung away. She said:

'He did it, didn't he?'

'That is another possibility.'

'But he must have done! I heard everything. And Dennys, he's just trying to throw Timothy a life-line.'

'You formed that opinion?'

'Don't play games with me! It was standing out a mile. And Dennys, he's just the sort to do it. Dennys rather likes Timothy.' She flicked Gently a look. 'You're pretty certain, aren't you? The way you summed it up didn't leave much doubt. All you need now is just a scrap of evidence, just something to place Timothy in the forest.'

'We require all relevant evidence.'

'You brute. You know very well what I mean.' Her eyes clung to his painfully. 'Tell me this. Is there a chance in a thousand of him getting off?'

'Getting off . . . ?'

'Yes! What you were saying. Irresistible impulse, wasn't it? It fits so well, if you know Timothy. That's how it would have happened, you can take my word for it.'

'Your brother is unstable?'

'I didn't say that! But you only have to know all that's happened, how he dropped out, the way he's living, these

– ' she swept her hand towards the pictures – 'these ridiculous attempts to do something with himself. Daddy is in despair about him – perhaps that's why Daddy fell so hard for Laurie! – and he's cut him to a strict allowance. Though Mummy tries to do something for him. You'll scarcely believe this, but Timothy thinks he's the crest of a new artistic wave, that he only has to be properly presented to become the new Francis Bacon or whatever. Shows in London, Paris and New York. That's what Timothy dreams about. It's pathetic. Then along comes Laurie, who Daddy worships and would buy the earth for.'

'And who turned the head of Miss Spinks.'

'Yes.' Her head bobbed emphatically. 'Though what Timothy sees in that silly little mommet is another thing again. I mean, there are tarts in Breckford who would think it glamorous to entertain Timothy, and perhaps some of them do. But no. He has to imagine himself in love with Spinky. Then Laurie grabs her too, and pastes Timothy into the bargain. And that's as much as Timothy can take. And that's when he goes for Hugh's gun.' She paused, a little breathless. 'Isn't that how it was – what in France they would call a *crime passionnel*? I mean, if he did it, which you haven't proved yet. Wouldn't he just be the victim of an irresistible impulse?'

Gently said: 'As you say, we lack proof.'

'And in the mean time – ' her mouth twisted – 'you're holding Hugh. And how nicely you spelled it out for me. I have to choose between brother and husband.'

Gently said: 'Do you have that choice?'

She turned away, stared at the pictures. 'You spelled that out for me too, didn't you?' she said. 'How the hell did you know where I rode on Sunday?'

Gently said nothing. After a moment, Cassandra Merton turned to face him again. Her mouth was still trembling as she said:

'All right. You bloody well win.'

'You did ride that way?'

She nodded. 'Mummy and I split up when we came to the brecks. She carried on up to the Heights, and we agreed to meet again at the old tank. I knew where Hugh was off to, of course. I thought I might see him if I went the forest way.'

'That being the track along the fringe of the forest.'

'Yes. You can follow it right through. And that's what I did, I rode through to the little dell, and hauled up there to see if I could spot him. From there, you can see quite a way down the ride, and a bit of the cross-ride to section 10.'

'And you saw your husband?'

'No! At first, I didn't see anyone at all. But I hung on for a few minutes, and then I saw someone coming up the ride. I gave him a wave, and he waved back. I was so certain it was Hugh. Then I saw it wasn't. It was Laurie. Laurie I did not wish to see. So I gave poor Brownie a whack and we cantered off over the brecks to join Mummy.'

Gently paused, said: 'And the shot?'

'That came at least five minutes later.'

'Then . . . you were virtually an eye-witness.'

'Don't be silly! I was probably a mile away by then. I'd joined Mummy, and Mummy was carrying on about peasants using guns on a Sunday. Of course, I realized the shot came from the forest direction, but I never connected it with Laurie, not even when he didn't turn up. Laurie simply wasn't popular with us.'

Gently said: 'Now tell me what else you saw.'

For some while, Cassandra Merton was silent.

Gently said: 'Was it your brother?'

She shook her head, her mouth twitching again.

'But – someone?'

Now she nodded. 'But I can't tell you who, I swear I can't! Just that . . . after what had happened between them . . . well, naturally, I thought of Timothy.'

'Describe what you saw.'

'Yes. It was just as I was turning Brownie to leave. I caught a glimpse of someone else down the ride. But he dodged out of sight. I couldn't tell who it was.'

'Some distance behind Laurence Stanton?'

'Oh yes. Perhaps a hundred yards behind him.'

'Too far for you to offer a description?'

'Yes. He was out of sight in a flash.'

'But – you thought of your brother.'

Cassandra Merton drew a deep breath. 'You brute. I've told you all I'm going to tell you now. And I'm jolly well not going to swear it was Timothy, when I couldn't tell who it was from Adam.'

'Not Timothy.'

Cassandra Merton glared at him.

'And not someone else.'

'Oh!'

The look should have killed him. It didn't. Cassandra Merton scrambled up and jumped ashore. She paused to spit before running up the path; and once more Gently was left in command of the houseboat.

7

He took the longer route back to the house, by way of the
Round Garden, which enabled him to check on the track
claimed to have been followed by Emma Spinks. The lie of
the land supported her story. Bush-willow and undergrowth concealed the track. She could have paused, come
and gone without attracting the attention of the pair at the
moorings; could have eaves dropped on the encounter,
should certainly have heard a tape being played, later. Had
she passed during one of Timothy Stanton's 'intervals'? Or
while he was absent on his alleged errand after water? In
the first case he could well have detected her presence,
passing with the dogs, though out of sight; and in the
second it was highly likely that she would run into him as
he left the house and she approached it. It followed that, at
four p.m. on Sunday, he was neither at the houseboat nor,
probably, engaged in the occupation he claimed . . .

The Round Garden was deserted, except for the even-
song of birds. Higher up, above the lawn and terrace, the
house still caught the last rays of sun. It looked comfortable
and domestic, simply a spacious family home, the porch its
only ostentation; a house that offered no challenge. Gently
paused briefly to admire it. Doubtless Warren Lodge was a
'railway house': a house in a situation which the coming of
the railway had rendered desirable. Hidden away behind
it, the big gallery would be a recent addition; otherwise,
little must have changed since the place was built in the

eighteen-fifties. Just that the trees had grown tall, while the forest had come to eat into the brecks, and cars now stood on the sweep where carriages and phaetons once had waited. A family house ... Shrugging, Gently continued his way towards it. On the steps of the porch, he found Phipps. The author watched his approach with disparaging eyes.

He said: 'If you don't mind, a word! I have been considering my rank as one of your suspects. Of course, I am honoured, but my unworthiness weighs on me. I feel the honour should go where the honour is due.'

Gently growled: 'Have you something to tell me?'

'Doubtless what you will regard as the merest trifle. But if you will step with me into the gallery, I will unfold my slender contribution.'

Gently gave him a stare, then nodded. Phipps led him down the hall and into the gallery. He searched among the switches, and flicked one; a light illuminated the Constable landscape. Phipps caressed his pointed beard. He said:

'Do you think you could put a value on that? Oh, I realize the market has slipped recently, but shall we say, within the nearest million?'

Gently said: 'Just get on!'

'I must make my point,' Phipps said. 'Our Gainsborough and Morland would also make you hesitate, and you may add our Turner, and possibly our Crome. But Constable is the name to conjure with. In the auction-room he reigns supreme. From New York and Tokyo the buyers flock in, with the press and the cameras hard on their heels. And this isn't just any old Constable. You may take it from me it is one of the gems. Its modest size is of small consequence: this is Constable at his zenith.'

'So?' Gently rapped.

'So.' Phipps sent a slanted glance at Gently. 'Let us

100

suppose we were to come across someone behaving suspiciously with regard to this painting. Let us suppose it was our late friend who observed this, and who made his suspicions exceeding plain. And let us set this drama on Sunday, a short while before that famous lunch. Admittedly I am no policeman, but in view of what followed, might we not allow that a certain interest obtains?'

After a pause, Gently said: 'You are accusing someone?'

'Heaven forbid!' Phipps drawled. 'Merely that, with suspicion going the rounds, I felt it only fair that it should be spread evenly. And so I rehearse these facts. You must make of them what you will.'

'So far, I haven't heard any facts.'

'Just testing the water,' Phipps said. 'Of course, if your mind is made up about Merton, I may as well not trouble you any further.'

'If you have any facts, let's hear them.'

'As long as I'm not boring you,' Phipps said. 'In short order, then. On Sunday morning I accompanied the deceased in here. I may say I was barely on terms with that gentleman, but we had an argument to settle about De Wint. When we entered, we were amazed to see that this picture had been taken down from the wall, and that the person responsible had it on a bench, where he was absorbed in studying the back of it. Laurence Stanton immediately accosted him and demanded to know what he was about. He replied with some feeble excuse about which Laurence Stanton expressed incredulity. The picture was rehung. Subsequently, at lunch, Laurence Stanton made meaningful remarks about the painting. He asked his father what its value might be, and advised him to check that it was fully insured. Sir Charles seemed surprised, while the person who had removed the painting kept his eyes on his plate.'

'And', Gently said, 'the name of that person?'

'Didn't I mention it?' Phipps said. 'Dennys Brewster.'

'Dennys Brewster!'

'So sorry,' Phipps said. 'I gather that I may have disappointed you.'

Gently gave him a long look. 'And the feeble excuse that he made to Stanton?'

'Oh, some triviality,' Phipps said. 'About camera angles, that sort of nonsense.'

'In short, he was photographing the painting?'

'That was the head and tail of his excuse.'

'He had his camera there?'

'Of course. Though it may have been merely window-dressing.'

'And this was suspicious?'

Phipps touched his beard. 'He could well have photographed it where it hung. A few more inches on the tripod, a stool fetched for him to stand on. One does not disturb Constables lightly. To take it down at all was an act of lese-majesty. But what we found him doing was examining the back of it, as might one with intentions less than avowable.'

'You suspected he had such intention?'

Phipps extended a hand. 'For myself, I merely report facts. But unquestionably the deceased indulged such thoughts, and had no hesitation in letting them appear. At lunch he was most explicit. I believe he meant to talk privately with his father afterwards. But then occurred the famous interruption, and the matter was thrust aside.'

'Ahem!' a third voice said.

They looked round: Dennys Brewster stood by the swing-doors.

'Do excuse me,' he said. 'But I caught a few words. Is it all right if I join in?'

Phipps drew himself up like an affronted peacock and stared witheringly at the intruder: Brewster merely grinned at him. He advanced to the picture, pretended to make a frame for it with his hands.

'The clue of the Unhung Constable!' he grinned. 'I was sure old Les was going to bring it up. When I saw him towing you in here, I knew my honour was about to be impugned. Did he make it convincing?'

Gently shrugged.

'Of course,' Brewster smiled. 'The idea has a certain grandeur. I mean, pinching a Stubbs would be purely criminal, but liberating a Constable is in a different league. The trouble is, I wouldn't have known what to do with it. I don't have many contacts in the art world.' He gave Phipps a knowing leer. 'I might have had to have gone to old Les for advice.'

'That is an insult!' Phipps hissed.

'Oh, I don't know,' Brewster smiled at Gently. 'Old Les is always in and out of the sale-rooms, he must have picked up connections here and there. Wouldn't you think?'

'You are a lout!' Phipps rasped. 'My integrity has never been questioned. But what I saw in here on Sunday was not simply a photographer going about his business. Why were you so interested in the back of that painting?'

Brewster shook his head in mock incomprehension. 'Wouldn't you have been interested in the back of a Constable? It's the first one I've ever had through my hands. Naturally, I wanted to see how the old boy had done things. That's a canvas he must have stretched himself.'

'Oh yes. And that's why you had it down – from a reverential interest in the painter?'

'Dearie me,' Brewster said. 'I thought I had explained that. I needed a flat-on angle for the camera.' He turned to Gently. 'May I be technical? I photographed the Constable first on Friday. But the best I could do was a tilt-angle, which left me with highlights on some of the brushwork. Well, that might do for a Bright or a Stanfield, but not for the pride of the collection. So Sunday morning I had a second shot, with the picture set up to give a flat-on angle.'

Gently said: 'You took that photograph?'

'But yes. Before the company arrived. It was afterwards they caught me in *flagrante delicto*, with conscious guilt oozing out of my ears.'

'Yes, treat it as a joke!' Phipps snapped. 'But that wasn't the way Laurence Stanton treated it.'

Brewster gave a comic shrug. 'So I went out and shot him. Of course. It was the obvious thing to do.' He sighed feelingly. 'And yet, as a motive, did it have a punch to equal yours? I feel that mine was too unlikely. I suppose it wasn't you with the gun, was it?'

'You', Phipps exploded, 'are quite despicable.'

'But you did have it in for him,' Brewster grinned. 'And here you are, trailing red herrings, as though you were afraid some mud was going to stick.'

'I won't listen to you!' Phipps snapped.

'No, perhaps it wasn't you either,' Brewster grinned. 'We'd best leave our friend here to decide. After all, that's what he's here for.'

Gently said: 'Just in passing! Neither of you two has a sustainable alibi. You might do better to stick together than to trouble the police with mutual recrimination.'

Phipps glared: Brewster made pretence of warding off a blow. Then Phipps turned smartly on his heel and marched out of the gallery.

'Oh dear,' Brewster said. 'Have we been very naughty?'

Gently eyed him. 'I'm not sure,' he said.

'Then we have. But it won't happen again, sir.'

Gently shrugged, and moved to turn off the light.

'Are you staying for dinner?'

In the hall he had found Sir Charles, chatting with Emma

Spinks. The latter cast him a resentful look before hurrying off in the direction of the study. Sir Charles steered him into the lounge, taking care to close the door behind them. He pulled together two of the club chairs, and motioned Gently to sit.

'You won't? Well, I can't say I blame you! This is scarcely the moment to press hospitality. Our Mr Phipps went by just now, looking like thunder, and Cassie has been swearing that someone should drown you. But that's not the point.' He drew his chair closer. For a moment he stared intently at Gently. 'Timothy,' he said. 'I've been talking to Timothy. Frankly, I must ask you to tell me where we stand.'

Gently said: 'Have you spoken to Miss Spinks?'

Solemnly, Sir Charles nodded. 'I understand she passed the moorings at around four, and cannot answer for Timothy then. Timothy is claiming he went up to the house, and that Mr Brewster saw him there. I haven't spoken to Mr Brewster, but I gather that you place little faith in what he says. Is this true?'

'I'm afraid it is.'

'Then Timothy's movements are entirely unconfirmed.'

'Entirely so.'

'And you suspect him in another matter – he wasn't very coherent – touching interference with a witness?'

'A witness who testified to meeting Hugh Merton.'

Sir Charles stared long, then his head sank. 'Perhaps you can appreciate my position! I have lost a son who was very dear to me, who cost my beloved first wife's life. I am still stunned by that tragedy. I can scarcely express what his return here meant to me. And now I am conscious of a nightmare shaping that I barely dare let myself contemplate. Can it be possible? I talked also to Cassandra, who related to me what she had overheard. From what she told me it seemed you had made your mind up, and were waiting only for additional confirmation. Is that true?'

Gently said: 'We are still at the stage of gathering information.'

'But you suspect Timothy?'

Gently said: 'In our view, it may lie between your son Timothy and your son-in-law.'

'It may lie?'

'As yet, our information is incomplete.'

'But you do suspect Timothy?'

After a pause, Gently said: 'Shall I say, we can't overlook him.'

Sir Charles's dark eyes dwelt on his. Then he shook his wiry head. 'I'm to blame! It was my folly that brought this terrible thing about. If the matter stands as you think it does, then it should be me who answers in the dock. I brought Timothy to this. I brought a son of mine to fratricide.'

Gently said: 'You were not responsible for the issue that arose between them.'

'Was I not? But would it have been such an issue, except for my extravagant behaviour? Girls have switched favours between brothers before, without it leading to bloody murder. But here it became the last straw, that which drove one of them over the edge.' He ran his hand through the dyed locks. 'You lack the background,' he said. 'You don't understand. Timothy was already in a state of alienation before Laurence ever turned up here. He was the youngest, and spoiled, you may think. His attitude was that life would always provide. At school, at university, and now, with his feeble pretence of being a painter. What was I to do? How treat him? I must admit to a certain intransigence. I found positions for him, urged him to reform, refused to accept his wilful idleness. It led nowhere, except to estrangement, and the sort of life he is living now. Along with this infatuation for my secretary, which she assures me she doesn't return.' Sir Charles gave his hair a smoothing

106

touch. 'And that, in brief, is the situation. I don't blame Emma. She's an agreeable girl, and Laurence would have turned any woman's head. But, for Timothy, Laurence was the devil. He was the prodigal, stealing all the birthright. The place I had never yielded to Timothy I was lavishing on this stranger from down-under. And then, he must claim Emma too. The alienation was complete.' He paused, looked questionably at Gently. 'Can you say now that I escape responsibility?'

Gently said: 'Your involvement was involuntary.'

'Involuntary.' Sir Charles caught at the word. 'And was Timothy's any other than involuntary, at that catastrophic moment down at the moorings? I think not. I think that if, indeed, he committed that dreadful deed, then it could only have been the involuntary act of one for whom despair had become finally complete. His responsibility had been destroyed. The devil had triumphed to the very last. He was in a state of involuntary response, and all that followed was an unreal dream. Could that not be so?'

Gently said nothing.

'Unlawful killing,' Sir Charles said. 'That must be the limit of any charge against him. Murder, manslaughter, neither are supportable, while the element of fratricide is nominal at the best. Would you not agree?'

Gently held the dark eyes. 'You have had an account from your son?' he said.

'An account – yes.'

'And he continues to maintain that he was nowhere else but at the moorings?'

'At the moorings – yes.'

'And is that all?'

Sir Charles drew back, very slightly. 'What are you suggesting?'

Gently said: 'As yet, we have no case against your son. A degree of suspicion, certainly, it may even be of strong suspicion. But no more. So you must expect my surprise at your apparent conviction in the matter.'

'Conviction – I?' The dark eyes had gone still.

'You seem to think it timely to outline his defence.'

'His defence? But that is hypothetical! I will not allow you to draw inferences from that.'

'It may be your information is better than mine.'

'No, sir. No. You must not suppose it.'

'Yet a son may confide in a father.'

'In so many words, sir, he has not confessed to me!'

'But . . . something short of a confession?'

'Upon my word,' Sir Charles said, 'I begin to think Cassie had a point! But you are doing your duty, I understand that, and I suppose I must congratulate you on it.'

'Then you have nothing to add?'

'I have not. My information is the same as your own. And if it seemed otherwise, my fear was speaking, for which I expect some allowance to be made.'

Gently gravely nodded.

Sir Charles said: 'Then I am to take it that is where we stand? You have no present case against my son, despite the suspicion you represent as attaching to him?'

Gently said: 'No present case.'

'And would the same not apply to my daughter's husband?'

Gently said: 'His position is perhaps more involved, and may take a little longer to elucidate.'

The eyes were shrewd. 'You mean you're nearer to a case there?'

Gently said: 'We are still seeking information.'

'Oh, very well, very well,' Sir Charles said. 'In your position I would be discreet too. But you will allow me to put in a word for Hugh. I have always found him a trustworthy fellow.'

Gently nodded. Then the door opened, and Lady Daphne rustled into the room.

She said: 'I've been talking to the children – and now I want a word with George!'

'George is just leaving, my dear,' her husband said quickly. 'I couldn't prevail on him to stay for the meal.'

'Well, he can't leave yet,' Lady Daphne said. 'Do you know, he's even been trying to involve Cassie? I propose to straighten dear George out – but first, I want a bloody drink!'

She went to the bar and poured herself a sherry. She had dressed for dinner, in a sage-green gown. She sipped her drink. Sir Charles placed a chair for her. She rustled across to it, sat, and adjusted her gown.

'Now,' she said. 'George. I don't care for that trick you played on Cassie. You knew full well she was listening in, and you deliberately set her up to make a frightful decision. She had either to shop Timothy or her husband, and now the poor girl doesn't know what she's done.'

'Oh, come now, Daphne,' Sir Charles said. 'Cassie had no right to be listening in the first place. George was perfectly in order to do what he did, and it got him information he should have had at the beginning.'

'Information my foot,' Lady Daphne said. 'It isn't worth tuppence to him anyway. But of course, you'll stand up for him, Charles. You and he share the same sort of background.'

'My dear, Cassie should have come clean from the start.'

'Don't make me laugh,' Lady Daphne said. 'Why should she get herself involved in this, when she had nothing worthwhile to contribute?'

'She didn't know that. We don't know that. It is for experts to evaluate information. And', Sir Charles said, carefully, 'it might have been more appropriate for all of us to have given our information freely.'

'Good lord.' Lady Daphne's eyes raked him. 'Is that intended for me?'

'I think you know what I mean, my dear. You could not but know which way Cassie had gone.'

'And I was to split on her?'

'In a case so grave, our petty loyalties cease to apply.'

'Now,' Lady Daphne said, 'I've heard just about everything. I'm being instructed to tell tales about my own daughter.' She quaffed waspishly. 'Then there's me. If Cassie was on the loose, so was I. Who knows what mischief I didn't get up to, and who I didn't see, and doing what.' She swung on Gently. 'Come on,' she said. 'I want to be given the third degree too. I was out there, not watching football. I deserve your attention along with the rest.'

'Daphne, Daphne!' Sir Charles chided.

'Oh no. I demand to be interrogated too.'

'You rode round the hills. You could have seen nothing.'

'That's just my tale. Why should anyone believe it?'

Sir Charles shook his head, stole a glance at Gently.

'George isn't saying a word,' Lady Daphne said. 'He just takes it all in. So perhaps he'd better take this in. Cassie really doesn't know who the fellow was she saw. She thought it might be Timothy, because of the row, but that's the only reason why. And I've just been having it out with Timothy, and you can take it from me there's nothing in it. So she saw someone. That's the length and breadth of it. And Timothy was never any nearer than the house.'

Sir Charles said: 'She could be sure it wasn't Hugh?'

'Oh!' Lady Daphne said. 'Wouldn't she know her own husband?'

'Just making the point,' Sir Charles said. 'I mean, it could still all have been an accident. I've been thinking –' he stole another glance at Gently – 'it's not impossible that Laurie took the gun out himself. That dell is a prime spot to lay for the bunnies, and if I were going that way I might pick up a gun.'

Lady Daphne stared at her husband. 'Ye-es,' she said. 'And then Hugh ran into him. And there was a row.'

'Very possible,' Sir Charles said. 'It was Hugh's gun, and Hugh didn't love Laurie. He could have tried to take it off him, and then it happened.'

'He could have thrown the gun aside.'

'Not unlikely. Then the gun went off and caught Laurie in the back.'

'And Hugh chased back here and put the gun in the gun-room.'

'He'd be in shock,' Sir Charles said. 'One couldn't really blame him.'

Lady Daphne's grey eyes narrowed. Sir Charles was looking firmly away from Gently. Lady Daphne drank, and put her glass down. At last she sighed, and shook her head.

'No,' she said. 'And do you know why?'

'I've known such things to happen,' Sir Charles said.

'But not with Hugh,' Lady Daphne said. 'If Hugh had done it, he would have admitted it. But he hasn't, and so he didn't, and that's that. End of story.'

'Yet . . . something of that sort could be the answer.'

Gently said: 'I'm holding up your meal. Perhaps I may use a telephone?'

'What?' Sir Charles said. 'Oh, damn it, man. I'll run you back myself.' He paused. 'No other questions?'

'Not just now,' Gently said.

'Use my car, Charles,' Lady Daphne said. 'There's really no need to get out the Bentley.'

Calthorpe had turned up another witness, a farmer, who had heard the shot, and, for what it was worth, had confirmed that Merton, on the Saturday, had shot a brace of rabbits at the Forestry Centre. He listened eagerly to what Gently had to tell him, especially to the admission by Cassandra Merton.

'You think it was him, sir, stalking Merton?'

'I think the odds may be it was Merton. But if so she will never testify against him, so we are still no further forward.'

Calthorpe pondered. 'You don't fancy Mr Timothy?'

After a pause, Gently shook his head. 'I'm not too certain about Mr Timothy! Except that he's a liar of the first order.'

'I'd say he bears watching, sir. If we can't make it stick with Merton. He's got it all going for him, and we're pretty certain it was him who tampered with Gourbold.'

'At the same time . . .' Gently gestured. 'Timothy Stanton is a spoiled boy. Like his sister, I think he knows something. But I'm not yet ready to hand him the gun.'

'It's plain he didn't stay on the houseboat, sir. And that stuff about containers has to be dodgy.'

'Yes . . . he didn't stay at the houseboat.'

'So where else would he have gone, sir – if it wasn't to the forest?'

Gently shook his head. 'We don't know! So we'll keep Mr Timothy in reserve. But Merton is still the man on the spot, and the man whose gun killed Laurence Stanton. So the pressure stays on Merton. That's the best we can do tonight.'

'And – tomorrow, sir?'

'Yes . . . tomorrow.' Gently played with an empty pipe. 'Tomorrow, I think we will indulge in a modest reconstruction. We'll take Merton into the forest.'

He left Calthorpe looking thoughtful, and went his way down to The Cross Keys. The sun was setting redly and throwing a glow on the glum flint houses. No one now was playing darts in the bar, but there was a buzz of

112

onversation among the regulars. Gently ordered a plate of sandwiches and ignored the looks that were being thrown him. While he ate and drank, he kept his eye on Timothy Stanton's painting; then, afterwards, he went out in the settling twilight to ring Gabrielle, from a box.

8

When they fetched Merton from the cell the next morning he was slouching in shoes from which the laces had been removed; Calthorpe produced the laces from a drawer, and with a bitter face the prisoner went about rethreading them. He looked up at Gently.

'Is this it, then?'

'We require your assistance, Mr Merton.'

'My what?'

'We are going to the forest to re-enact your movements on the Sunday afternoon.'

The blue eyes rounded, then were suddenly afraid. 'But why? What on earth is that going to tell you?'

'It may help us to fill in some gaps. To extend our information.'

'But suppose I don't want to do it?'

'You don't wish to co-operate?'

He stared around wretchedly at his captors. Then he shut his mouth grimly and stood, head bowed, resigned to the fate they were proposing.

Calthorpe drove. Bodney went with them, sitting in the back of the car with Merton. It was another idyllic June morning, with the sun exquisite on tree and building. As they crossed the bridge, Calthorpe murmured to Gently:

'Do we take him in by the back way, sir?'

Gently shook his head. 'Straight up the drive, and park on the sweep in front of the house.'

114

Calthorpe stared, but did as he was bidden. They turned in through the gryphon-guarded gates. As they approached the sweep, he hesitated, but then continued, to park almost opposite the steps. They got out. Just for a moment, their arrival appeared unobserved; the next, Sir Charles came hastening down the steps, his hand held out towards the unhappy Merton.

'Hugh! It's all over, then? They realize they've made a mistake?'

He grabbed Merton's limp hand and pumped it, then seemed to realize that perhaps all was not quite well. He peered at Gently.

'You've done with him, have you?'

Gently said: 'Mr Merton is still giving us his assistance.'

'Assistance! But he's been doing that since yesterday. You must have done with the poor fellow by now.'

'I regret there is still ground to be covered.'

'Ground – what ground?' Sir Charles began, then there came a wild cry from the house, and Cassandra Merton vaulted down the steps and ran towards them. She threw herself into Merton's arms.

'Hugh – Hugh! They had to let you go, then.'

'The devil, that's just what they haven't!' Sir Charles snorted. 'According to George, he's still stuck with it.'

'But he can't be!' She drew back her head and stared at Merton's miserable face. 'Hugh – everything is all right, isn't it? Speak to me, Hugh. Speak to me!'

Merton tried, but nothing came out. Cassandra Merton turned furiously on Gently.

'You brute – you rotten brute! You know, you must know he didn't do it.'

'Hush, Cassie!' Sir Charles pleaded.

'But he knows – and still he's going on with it.'

'There has to be a reason,' Sir Charles said.

'There isn't, Daddy – there isn't – there isn't!'

She grabbed Merton and sobbed on his chest. Now they

115

were joined by Lady Daphne, while Phipps, and then Brewster, had come out on the steps. Finally, Emma Spinks appeared hesitatingly in the porch. But of Timothy Stanton there was no sign. Lady Daphne pulled her daughter away from Merton.

'Stop it, girl! Stop making an exhibition.'

'But they think he's done it, Mummy. They really do!'

'That's no cause for you to expose yourself. Be quiet, girl, and dry your eyes.'

'He won't speak to me!'

'That's scarcely surprising. Now pull your foolish self together.'

Cassandra Merton sniffled, and stood staring at her husband with wide, almost resentful eyes. Merton hung his head and kept his eyes on the gravel; so far, he hadn't managed a word.

'Now. What's this all about?' Lady Daphne demanded. 'Why have you brought my son-in-law here?'

'That', Sir Charles said, 'was what I was attempting to discover when Cassie burst upon the scene.' He turned to Gently. 'Perhaps you will explain, and without the routine circumlocutions. If you have business here with Hugh, then I think I am entitled to be advised.'

Gently inclined his head. 'My apologies if we have created any disturbance!'

'Never mind that, George! Why are you here, and what are you intending to do with Hugh?'

Gently said: 'Your son-in-law has been helpful, but the events of Sunday are still not quite clear. We think it may help to remove some uncertainties if he took us over his movements with regard to the forest.'

Sir Charles stared hard. 'Uncertainties?'

'With particular reference to routes and timing.'

'You mean – he hasn't been frank about that?'

'We feel a re-enactment may be helpful.'

Cassandra Merton set up a wail. 'He thinks I saw Hugh

there!' she cried. 'I didn't, Hugh, it may have been Timothy, but I had to tell him, and now he's certain it was you.'

'Quiet, girl!' Sir Charles rapped. But Hugh Merton's head had jerked up. Now he was staring at his wife with aghast, unbelieving eyes. He croaked:

'You couldn't have done – you couldn't!'

'No, I didn't Hugh – I swear! But I saw someone, and I had to tell him. The rotten brute trapped me into it.'

'But you were nowhere near – '

'Yes.' Her head was nodding uncontrollably. 'I rode round that way, I thought I might see you, but it was Laurence who I saw.'

'Laurence!'

'Yes – I saw him. He was coming up the ride. And someone else, a long way behind him, too far for me to see who it was.'

'Too far . . .'

'Yes, too far! And he dodged out of sight straight away.'

Sir Charles snarled: 'That's enough, and I mean it!'

But the despair in Hugh Merton's eyes was plain to see.

Sir Charles said to Gently: 'Very well, then. A fool would understand your business now. I think you are mistaken, but that's beside the point. You come with a purpose, and you had best pursue it.' He took Merton's hand again. 'Hugh. Keep your spirit up, old man. None of us here believe it of you. Don't let these people get you down.'

But Merton was gazing at his wife.

'Oh Hugh, Hugh!' Cassandra Merton wailed. Her mother took her arm. She said:

'Come, girl. You've let yourself down enough for one morning.'

'But I can't just leave him!'

'We will go in.'

'Oh, no!'

But Lady Daphne was adamant. She led her tearful daughter back to the steps, where the three spectators in

117

the scene made way for them. Sir Charles gave Gently a meaningful stare, then turned on his heel and followed the others. Emma Spinks vanished; Phipps said something to Brewster, Brewster shrugged. And then the stage was empty.

'Phew!' Calthorpe whistled softly. He made a pretence of wiping his brow. 'We did ask for it, sir!'

'Bring Merton,' Gently said to Bodney.

Rhododendrons, red, orange and purple, concealed the path that wound its way towards the forest, and which was joined by a second path, presumably that from the Round Garden. The distance was not great; one was quickly aware of the reef of pines above the bright-flowered shrubs; and then abruptly, on turning a corner, one arrived at the smartly varnished field-gate, equipped with a spring to close it and with a sturdy spring catch. The party halted. Gently said to Merton:

'Did you use this gate on Sunday?'

'You know I did!'

'Open it now.'

Merton hesitated, as though suspecting a trick, then smoothly, familiarly, depressed the catch. The gate swung back silently, on well-oiled hinges, and Merton held it against the spring while they passed through; then, just as familiarly, he eased it shut, depressing the catch to locate it.

'Open it again, and let it slam.'

'But that way you can damage the latch!'

'Just do it.'

Pettishly, Merton obeyed, and the result was a resounding thud.

'Are you happy now?'

Calthorpe caught Gently's eye – two thuds had been reported by Phipps on the Sunday. If Merton had not been one of the thudders, then, by inference, they had a spare chummie . . .

Gently said: 'When you passed here on Sunday, you were unaware of the presence of any other person?'

'If you mean Laurence, yes, I was. I didn't see him or anyone else.'

'And you heard nothing? Say the slam of this gate?'

'I heard it slam when the horses went through.'

'But after that?'

'No, I didn't. So if Laurence slammed it, I was some-where else.'

Gently stared, then shrugged, and waved towards the ride. They moved on into the fragrance of the trees. Grim-faced, Merton went with Bodney at his shoulder, with Gently and Calthorpe a pace or two behind. The forest was quiet in its morning coolness. A few butterflies rose from the patches of sunlight. Afar off one could hear the tapping of a woodpecker, the soft crooning of a pigeon. Then Calth-orpe touched Gently's arm.

'Sir, I'm getting the impression we're being followed!'

'Yes.' Gently had heard it too, the occasional rustle, some distance behind them.

'Do you want me to investigate?'

Gently shook his head. 'You may frighten them off.'

'The trouble is, there's too much cover here!'

'So let them play games. Till they make a mistake.'

They came to the rough cross-ride of Merton's statement, but Merton passed it without a glance. There was sweat on the averted face, determination in the thrust of the jaw. Gently didn't halt him. The next cross-ride was that which Gourbold claimed to have taken. It occurred where the main ride commenced on a shallow gradient, and there Gently did pull them up. To Bodney, he said:

'You go ahead, and wait for us at the top of the rise.'

Merton mopped sweat. He jerked at Gently:

'Is this where that lout says he saw me?'

Gently didn't reply. Bodney strode away; he came to the summit of the gradient, and paused. Against a background of bracken and receding trees his figure stood out boldly, as would a stick or a gun, had he carried either. Gently glanced at Merton.

'Any comment?'

'Yes! I've already admitted he may have seen me.'

'Just that?'

Merton glared at him, and stuck out his jaw a bit further. Calthorpe, meanwhile, had been covertly observing the ride along which they had come. He frowned, and shook his head at Gently: their stalker had made no mistake, as yet.

'Let's go.'

From the brow of the gradient the birches of the dell showed plainly ahead, then, as they progressed, a glimpse of the brecks, with a broader sky lifting above them. To the left, the ultimate cross-ride bore away towards section 10, while the main ride ended there: at the junction, and at the dell. As they approached it, Gently halted them again. He said to Merton:

'We'll follow you. As nearly as you can remember, I want you to follow the same course as on Sunday.'

'I can't remember precisely!'

'Try.'

'And if I get it wrong, will that do for me?'

'Just do your best.'

'Oh hell!' Merton snapped, and set off up the ride at almost a trot.

In fact, he had few options; the track along the ride was hemmed with undergrowth. Bramble, bracken and snowberry, it brought him relentlessly to the mouth of the dell. As he neared it, he sought a diversion by wading and trampling through bracken, but brambles fetched him back to the track; to go that way, one must pass by the dell.

'That will be far enough.'

120

Merton halted, breathless, at the psychological point on the track. Gently moved up beside him. From there, one was looking into the shallow basin of the dell, with the brecks beyond it. Birches enclosed it, ground cover clothed it, then there was the stubborn fortress of the holly; but, from the height of a man, most of that declivity was in view.

'Sergeant.'

Bodney joined them.

'I want you to take up position in there.'

'Where we found him, sir?'

'Where you found him.'

'Right you are, sir,' Bodney said.

'But that isn't fair!' Merton exclaimed. 'He could put himself anywhere in there.'

'Don't you worry, sir,' Bodney said. 'There'll still be some bloodstains where he lay.'

'But – !'

'The way he bled, sir, it won't be washed out for a few days yet.'

Merton stared at him, mouth gaping, a pallor growing under the sweat. Bodney dived zestfully into the dell, dodging round brambles and hedges of snowberry. He came to the spot, stood thoughtful for a moment, then eased himself to the ground; they heard a rustling as he aligned himself, saw a hand thrust out and allowed to sink.

'Reckon this is it, sir!'

Almost, not quite, Bodney was hidden by the bracken and snowberry: a foot, shod in a trainer, projected, and the out-thrust hand gleamed palely. Gently said quietly:

'Well?'

'I swear, I swear I didn't see him!'

'He might still have been alive.'

'No!'

'He could have been groaning. Still capable of movement.'

'No – no!'

121

'How could you have missed him?'

'I – !'

'Didn't you admit that you heard the gunshot?'

'But that was over there!'

'Wouldn't it have alerted you, made you a little curious about what was happening here?'

'People are always shooting – '

'On a Sunday?'

'I tell you, I didn't think anything of it! When I came by here, all I was thinking about was getting in a wash before tea.'

'You wouldn't have seen that hand? That foot?'

'No!'

'Or heard your brother-in-law groan?'

'Oh my God, no, no!' Merton was trembling, swaying a little.

Gently said to the brecks: 'Isn't it possible that you didn't come by here at all – that you never went to section 10? That you never went further than this very spot?'

'I did – I did!'

'Yet you missed seeing the body?'

'Stop it, stop it!' a fresh voice cried. 'It was me – I who killed him!'

And Cassandra Merton rushed out from behind the holly.

Gently said: 'Ah, Mrs Merton. I was expecting you to join us.'

'Brute. Brute!'

She had flung Calthorpe aside, and rushed to grab the arm of her tottering spouse. From his bushes, Bodney had risen from the dead, and stood staring at her in amazement.

'You knew, didn't you? You knew all along! All this was just to get me to confess. Just like yesterday – it was all part of it – part of your rotten, lousy method!' She breathed fiercely. 'So now you've succeeded, and now you can stop persecuting Hugh. Because it was me. I shot Laurence. Big deal – George Gently does it again!'

Gently said: 'You are disturbed, Mrs Merton.'

'Yes – and who has just done the disturbing?'

'Perhaps, if you calmed down – '

'Now, he tells me!'

' – we could discuss your contribution more profitably.'

'Big man, big man!' She turned to Merton. 'It's all right now, Hughie. It's all over. I did it. I shot Laurence. Though of course, I never meant to tell them.'

'But – but – '

'It's all over! I know, I ought to have told you before. But you can't go blabbing a thing like that, not even to your husband. Then there's Daddy. He'll be so wild. And Mummy won't think so much of it, either. But you do understand, Hughie. For your sake I had to come out with it.'

If Merton was tottering before, now his condition was pathetic. He gazed at his wife with horrified eyes, seemed with one hand to be feeling for support.

'But – you couldn't have!'

'Oh yes, I could.'

'No.' He shook his head rapidly. 'You were with Mother, remember? You were with her when she heard the shot.'

'That was a tale.'

'But Mother – !'

'She told it to keep me out of trouble. She didn't know I'd shot Laurence, of course. Just that I wasn't around at the time.'

'I still can't see – '

'So listen, you schmuck.' Cassandra Merton flashed a look at Gently. 'I did ride round this way, and I did see Laurence back down the ride there. And I saw something else. He had a gun. And it was a gun that looked like yours. So I thought I'd have a word with Master Laurence, and I got down and hitched Brownie to a fence-post.'

'*He* had my gun!'

'Yes, imbecile. You didn't think I went out with it, did you? I thought it was a bit of cheek, and I climbed over the fence to have it out with him.'

'I won't believe this!'

'Just listen. I told him he'd no right to take your gun. And he laughed at me. And that made me mad. So I snatched the gun from him. And that's when it happened.'

'No – it couldn't have!'

'Yes, it did.'

'But he was shot . . . he was shot in the back.'

'Yes.' She nodded. 'I gave him a shove, and he pitched forward on his face. Then the gun went off in my hands. That's how he got it in the back.'

'The gun . . . just went off?'

'Yes. Heaven knows how it happened. And there he lay. And it was your gun. And I knew you were somewhere in the forest.' She flashed another look at Gently. 'So what was I to do? Oh, I was shocked about Laurence and all that, but it didn't help, I had to get that gun back, and then I had to pick up Mummy on the brecks. So that's what I did. I galloped home like fury, and shoved the gun back on its rack. Then I galloped off to join Mummy, and spun her some yarn about watching crossbills.' She paused. 'And now it's off my chest. And they can stop playing their games with my husband.'

Merton stared at her with hazy eyes. 'And you would go through with all this . . . just for me?'

'Damn it, yes. What are wives for?'

He looked, then very slowly shook his head. 'It won't do, Cassie.'

'But Hughie, that's what happened!'

124

'No.' He went on shaking his head. 'It's a brave try. But they won't believe you.'

'I'll swear to it, Hughie!'

'It won't do.'

'Hughie!'

And suddenly the fire went out of her. She clung to Merton with all her might, her face pressed to him, her shoulders heaving. Bitterly, Merton faced Gently. He said:

'She nearly got it right. Just one little thing wrong. It was me who took the gun from Stanton.'

'Oh Hughie, no!' Cassandra Merton sobbed. 'He's trying to protect me, don't you see?'

Merton patted her back. 'It was me you saw, Cassie. Me who was following Laurence out here. I wanted to talk to him about the cottage, then when I caught up with him, I saw he had my gun.'

'Don't believe him. It isn't true!'

'My gun,' Merton said. 'He'd no right to take it. We keep a spare one there for the guests, and I wasn't going to have him using mine.'

'He's lying, lying!'

Merton patted her back. 'The rest went the way she was pretending. There was a struggle, and Stanton went sprawling, and I must have caught my finger on a trigger.'

'No, it wasn't him. It was me!'

Merton tried to keep his gaze fixed on Gently's. 'I know I did wrong, but I couldn't face it, not telling Sir Charles I'd shot his son. So I did what I did. I put the gun back. I was in too much of a state to clean it. Then I hung about in the shrubberies until it was time to show up for tea. And that's it. You've been right all along. I never did go to section 10.'

'Oh, Hughie, Hughie, Hughie!'

'Now you've got it all,' Hugh Merton said.

125

His wife sobbed, Merton hugged her; Bodney was still staring from the bushes. Calthorpe had moved a little closer, was quizzing the couple with narrowed eyes. Gently said:

'And neither one nor other of you thought of fetching help for Laurence Stanton?'

'He was dead,' Merton jerked. 'What was the sense of fetching help?'

'Laurence Stanton bled to death.'

'He was dead – he was dead when he hit the ground!'

Gently shook his head. 'And furthermore, the pattern of the shot shows he was shot at a distance of about twelve feet.'

'But . . . that's not possible!'

'And shot deliberately.' Gently surveyed the pair mildly. 'So now, which one of you two would prefer to take the blame?'

Cassandra Merton had broken away from her husband, and stood staring with hot eyes. But before she could speak the scene was interrupted by the rapid thud of approaching hoof-beats, and Lady Daphne cantered into view, astride a handsome grey, going sixteen hands. She reined in.

'So what the devil's going on here?'

'Oh Mummy, I'm so glad you've come!' Cassandra Merton cried. 'I told them I shot Laurie, but they won't believe me, and now poor Hughie has gone and confessed!'

'Confessed? What rubbish!' Lady Daphne said. 'George, pay no attention to these silly children.' She slid from the saddle and tossed the reins to Calthorpe. 'I shot the Aussie myself,' she said.

'Take a look at that.'

In breeches and habit, she strutted up to confront Gently.

What her crop was pointing to was a leathern device secured to her saddle.

'You've seen one before, have you? It's a holster to take your shooter. Just the job in this sort of country, where there's a rabbit under every blade of grass. And I took a gun on Sunday – Hugh's, I knew he wouldn't mind. I dare say Cassie never noticed, it's something I'm doing all the time.'

Cassandra Merton caught her breath. But said nothing.

Gently said: 'Then you were the rider who came this way?'

'Of course I was. Don't pay any attention to the tales that Cassie comes out with. I was riding by when I spotted the Aussie, and I hauled up to give him a piece of my mind. I mean, at lunch he was egging Timmy on, deliberately flirting with that daft little Emma. He deserved a telling off, and that's what I intended to give him.'

'He was on this side of the fence, and you on the other?'

'Yes. I called him over to talk to him. But when he heard what I had to say, he just gave a grin, and started to walk off. Well, I wasn't going to have that, so I hopped down to go after him. And that was it. My habit caught in the twelve-bore, swung it round and fired it off. I tell you, I thought I'd shot myself, but then I saw I'd shot him. It bowled him over like a rabbit. For a moment I couldn't believe my eyes.'

Gently said: 'So what did you do?'

'Good lord, what would you expect me to do? I hitched Beauty, got over the fence, and went to give him a hand up.'

'He was – still conscious?'

'Could have been. Could have been I'd merely winged him. But as soon as I saw where it had got him, I knew it was all up. He was dead, a dead bird, not a breath left in him.'

'Oh Mummy, Mummy!' Cassandra Merton wailed.

'Just hold your tongue, girl,' Lady Daphne flung at her. 'George has heard enough silliness from you. So hold your tongue, and don't interrupt me.'

Cassandra Merton held her tongue.

Gently said: 'You were content with your diagnosis?'

'Of course.' She threw him a sharp look. 'I'm an experienced shot, please bear in mind. I've seen plenty of dead animals.'

'No question, then?'

'None. The least sign, and I'd have ridden for help. But it wasn't on. The Aussie was a dead man. So then I had to consider my own position. I had just shot the son of my husband, and that's what I would have to report to the police. Not an appealing prospect, was it? When Charles had made such a production over him.'

'So, you didn't.'

'You're so right. I stuffed that gun back in the gun-room. Then I rode out to pick up Cassie, who mentioned hearing a shot. I said I'd heard one too.'

'Oh, *Mummy!*' Cassandra Merton groaned.

Lady Daphne stunned her with a look. 'Later, of course, we had to square our stories, but that's all Cassie has ever known about it.' She flicked her crop. 'Any more you want to know?'

Gently said: 'Why did you wipe the gun?'

'Didn't.' She held her hands out. 'Gloves. Didn't think to use a pull-through on it, worst luck.'

Gently was beginning: 'Would it just be possible . . .', when the grey whinnied violently, and made a frisk: one of Calthorpe's DCs had come panting up the ride, seemingly with urgent tidings to be told. He dodged round the grey. He panted to Gently:

'Sir, you're wanted back at the house! According to this Mr Phipps, one of the pictures has gone missing from the gallery.'

'One of the pictures . . .?'

128

'That's right, sir.'

'Would you happen to know which one?'

'Says to tell you it's the Constable.'

'God's bloody pyjamas!' exclaimed Lady Daphne. 'Then that's five big ones gone up the spout.'

9

Lady Daphne climbed back on the grey and quickly cantered out of sight; twenty minutes later, when the others
arrived at the house, they found the grey hitched to a rail
outside. Gently halted them on the sweep. To the DC he
said:

'Escort Mr Merton to the station, then return here.'

'No, you can't!' Cassandra Merton cried. 'If you're going
to arrest him, you must take me too.'

'I may require you here, Mrs Merton.'

'But – !'

Gently nodded to the DC, who touched Merton's arm.
Merton gave his wife a long look, then allowed himself to
be guided to a car. Cassandra Merton stood clenching and
unclenching her hands while he got in the car, and was
driven away. Then she burst out:

'You brutes – you brutes! You know now he didn't do it.'

'Shall we go in?'

'But you know. You know.'

Then she turned, and raced up the steps ahead of them.

The swing-doors to the gallery were pegged open, and
inside it every light was switched on. Sir Charles, his lady
and Emma Spinks formed one little group; Phipps, Brewster and Timothy Stanton another. Then there was a DC
hovering by the doors, looking embarrassed and as though
he felt out of place: before he could stop her, Cassandra

Merton rushed past him and threw herself into her mother's arms.

'Oh Mummy, Mummy, Mummy!'

'Behave yourself, you stupid girl.'

'But they've taken Hughie away again!'

'If you can't be quiet, you must go to your room.'

Meanwhile, Gently had advanced to stare blankly at the space on the wall, from which, if the Constable had ever been missing, it clearly was not missing now. *The Grange Farm, Woolpit*: J. Constable' continued to occupy its place of honour. Sir Charles cleared his throat, said:

'This is all rather awkward, George. But Mr Phipps seems so positive that I felt bound to have you informed.'

Gently said: 'Had the painting been removed?'

'Not exactly removed,' Sir Charles said. 'In fact, I am in doubt if anything is amiss. But Mr Phipps is a greater expert than myself, and I suppose we must give his opinion due attention. Mr Phipps?'

Leslie Phipps gave Gently his supercilious stare. Then he slowly raised his hand and pointed to the picture. He said:

'That painting has been switched.'

'Switched . . .?'

'That is my considered opinion. The original has been removed and an expert copy substituted. Furthermore, the switching occurred at some time after seven p.m. yesterday, when I was last in the gallery, and when the original was certainly in place. I paid it particular attention because of a recent incident.'

'Oh dear!' Brewster murmured. 'The Unhung Constable!'

Phipps threw him a scathing look. He said: 'Note, I am making no insinuations. Simply stating what, in my opinion, is a fact, namely that the picture before us is a very clever fake.'

Sir Charles viewed the painting with narrowed eyes. 'Oh, I don't know, Leslie,' he said. 'I've lived with that

131

canvas for twenty years, and it looks like the genuine article to me.'

'But, in my view, it is not.'

'How can you tell, man?'

Phipps paused, then stepped closer to the painting. He extended a delicate finger and let it home in on an area of foliage.

'The brushwork, here. It is too studied. Constable's touch is more confident. Then you will notice the varnish-bloom, here. That bloom was absent from the original canvas. No doubt there are other pointers, but these two alone would be sufficient evidence.'

Sir Charles shook his head. 'Doesn't seem much to me!'

'But you, as you allow, are not an expert.'

'But I am familiar with that picture. I'd swear it was the one they knocked down to me at Sotheby's.'

'Perhaps you bought a fake,' Timothy Stanton grinned. 'Two hundred thou – wasn't that what you gave for it?'

Brewster said: 'Perhaps we could have it down to look at the back, and see if it is the same as I was looking at on Sunday.'

'Yes, take it down,' Sir Charles said, with a quelling glance at his son. 'Since we've brought George in on this, we had better leave no stone unturned.'

With a contemptuous shrug, but with infinite care, Phipps lifted the picture from the wall, carried it to one of the benches and propped it up with its back towards them. He, Brewster and Sir Charles studied it. The darkened canvas was clearly in period.

'That's it,' Brewster said. 'To the best of my memory.'

'Looks the same to me,' Sir Charles said.

Phipps said icily: 'No faker in his right mind would use other than a canvas of that era. They select a worthless contemporary daub and execute their work over it.' He bent closer to the painting. 'Look . . . these tacks have come out recently!' He pointed to the frieze of panel pins employed to secure the painting in the frame. 'You can see, some of them are bent. And some are showing bright metal, where they have been hammered.' He turned triumphantly to Sir Charles. But Sir Charles was shaking his head.

'It won't do, Leslie. We had the cleaners in the fortnight before Easter. I superintended the work myself, and it was they who had the painting out of its frame.'

'But . . . this is more recent!'

'It won't do.' Sir Charles turned abruptly to Gently. He said: 'I begin to feel I owe you an apology, George, for summoning you back here so peremptorily. I suppose you wouldn't be familiar with this line of country?'

Gently shrugged. To Brewster, he said: 'Didn't you photograph this painting on Sunday?'

'Absolutely right!' Brewster exclaimed. 'I should have thought of it before.'

'You have a print prepared?'

'Yes indeed. And I could blow you up a big one.'

'Just the print you have to hand.'

Brewster ducked his head and hastened out.

'Tally-ho!' Timothy Stanton smirked. 'Now we shall see what our Leslie is worth. If that print proves this is the picture, that's one reputation up for grabs.'

'Silence, boy,' Sir Charles rapped. 'Even the best of us can make mistakes.'

'At the same time, Charles,' Lady Daphne said, 'this is not the sort of mistake that one appreciates.'

Phipps, meanwhile, had drawn himself tall, and was staring ahead with affronted eyes; Cassandra Merton still clung to her mother's arm; Emma Spinks had her frightened gaze on Timothy Stanton.

Brewster returned. He handed Gently a manilla envelope, then deftly reversed and propped up the painting. From the envelope Gently drew a print still redolent with developing fluid, which he placed alongside the painting.

133

They gathered round it. Phipps's eyes were savage as they switched from print to painting, from painting to print. Brewster was grinning, Timothy Stanton smirking, Sir Charles staring with indignant eyes. Lady Daphne swept the exhibits with a lofty gaze, and she it was who finally gave voice.

'Correct me if I am wrong, but do I hear an apology from a certain person?'

'Oh, give him time, Mother!' Timothy Stanton giggled. 'It's an awful long way from his perch to the ground.'

'That print and the picture are identical.'

'I must say it looks like it,' Sir Charles frowned. 'Even that bit of bloom there he was talking about. And the foliage too. I can't see any difference.'

'I could blow it up some more,' Brewster offered.

'Be a waste of time,' Timothy Stanton said. 'It's too obvious. Our Leslie has dropped one from a great height.'

Very slowly, Phipps straightened up from his scrutiny. 'They are *not* identical,' he said. 'Because they can't be. And neither are they. That is my opinion. The resemblance merely flatters the skill of the forger.'

'Oh, come on, Les,' Brewster urged. 'An honest mistake and all that.'

'I am not mistaken. That is not the painting that hung in the gallery yesterday evening.'

'Well, it hung there on Sunday.'

'It did not.'

'You mean you won't withdraw?' Sir Charles frowned.

'I will not withdraw,' Phipps said. 'You have my opinion, and I maintain it, in the teeth of the hilarity of some of those present. During last night that painting was switched, and you will do well to give the matter your attention. I cannot allow the photograph as proof, however close you may find the resemblance.'

Whereupon with extravagant dignity, Phipps stalked out of the gallery.

'Well, the silly ass!' Lady Daphne exclaimed. But her husband had a troubled expression. He said:

'This is probably a storm in a teacup, George, but one can't play fast and loose with property like a Constable. What do you think?'

Gently said: 'Last night, were the monitors switched on?'

Sir Charles shook his head. 'We only use them on open days. The house security takes care of the rest.'

'But that was in operation?'

'Oh yes.'

'Perhaps we should give it a once-over, sir,' Calthorpe piped up. 'A routine check, sir. I know the system. You've had me out here before.'

'If you would do that, I should be grateful.'

'We can check for break-ins at the same time, sir.'

Sir Charles handed Calthorpe a bunch of keys, and the local man and his two colleagues departed. Reverentially, Sir Charles picked up the painting and hung it once more on the wall. He remained gazing at it for a moment.

'What a fool I would be if Leslie were right!'

'Don't be absurd, Charles,' his wife said. 'I've known that painting quite as long as you, and there's no question but it is the right one.'

'Leslie is a leading expert.'

'After this morning, I beg leave to doubt it. Either that, or he's stirring things up just to show what a great man he is.'

'I wish I could believe that,' Sir Charles sighed. Then he turned again to Gently. 'Please bear with me! All this must seem mere vanity compared with the reason you are here.'

Gently bowed his head. 'Perhaps, a coincidence.'

'I would give twenty Constables to have Laurence back here.'

Lady Daphne gave Gently a sidelong look: Cassandra Merton's hand tugged at her mother's arm. But just then Calthorpe reappeared to hand back Sir Charles's bunch of keys.

135

'All in order, Inspector?' Sir Charles said.

'All in order, sir. And my men are checking the outside now. But, sir – ' Calthorpe looked awkwardly at Gently – 'something does occur to me, sir, if what Mr Phipps was saying is right.'

'Yes, Inspector?'

'It's like this, sir. If that picture was switched overnight, and if there's no sign of any break-in, then likely the real one is still in the house.'

Sir Charles's eyes narrowed. 'You mean an inside job?'

'Always supposing Mr Phipps is right, sir.'

'And you want to search the house?'

'That would be routine, sir.'

Sir Charles stared long, then shook his head. 'I don't think we should go that far, Inspector. Not as the matter stands at present. We would need to be more certain of the fact before we allowed such suspicion as you suggest.'

'Of course, it's up to you, sir,' Calthorpe said, dashed.

Sir Charles frowned. 'What do you say, George?'

Gently pointed to the picture. 'It rests with that. And as yet, we have only one man's opinion.'

'As yet?' Sir Charles's eyes were sharp.

'We have an expert available at Scotland Yard.'

'At Scotland Yard . . .'

'Oh dear!' Brewster grinned. 'Our Les has really opened up a can of worms.'

Reluctantly Sir Charles gave his consent, and Gently made his phone call from the study. Seymour, the Fraud Squad's leading art expert, was available and would take the next train down. Meanwhile the gallery was vacated and its doors carefully locked by Sir Charles; and at long last the impatient grey was led back to the stables, to be unsaddled and stalled by the outside-man, Stringer. It was then that Lady Daphne tackled Gently.

'Don't we have some unfinished business?'

She caught him on the steps, as he was on his way to rejoin Calthorpe. Determinedly, she ushered him back into the hall, then down a passage to a small boudoir, one furnished with blue drapes and in which the only picture was a Paul Nash.

'Like some coffee?'

She lifted a house-phone, and shortly Jenny, the housemaid, appeared with a tray. Jenny poured, and handed the cups; then was dismissed with an impatient wave. Lady Daphne fixed her grey eyes on Gently.

'Now. Let's try to get this affair in focus. You want to clear it up with the fewest tears shed – that's the reason you were sent here, isn't it?'

Gently drank coffee.

'Yes,' Lady Daphne said. 'The fewest tears. So let's bear that in mind. And it can't be done by harassing the silly children, or pushing Hugh around till he blurts. No. You need a stronger character. Someone who can take it on the chin. And now you've got one. You've got me. I'm your woman. I shot Laurence.'

Gently drank coffee.

'Are you hearing me?' Lady Daphne said.

'Yes, I'm hearing you,' Gently said.

Lady Daphne's eyes were mean. 'No doubt you're thinking of Cassie,' she said. 'Well, you can put Cassie out of the reckoning. She said what she did merely to protect me. She wasn't there. She knew that I was. She guessed I'd taken that gun along. So she gave you that cock-and-bull story about seeing Laurence being followed by a man. Do you understand now?'

Gently nodded.

'Then perhaps we're getting somewhere,' Lady Daphne said. 'Really, we can work this thing out sensibly, with a little good will on both sides. It means a shock for Sir

137

Charles, of course, but I'm sure he will appreciate the position I was in. And I suppose I'll get a wigging for not reporting it. But I promise you, I can take that in my stride.'

Gently drank coffee. He said: 'Then you're going through with it?'

'To the hilt,' Lady Daphne said. 'You can depend on me.'

'That you shot Laurence Stanton in the way you described?'

'Right,' Lady Daphne said. 'Any magistrate around here will accept that.'

'And that Laurence Stanton fell dead?'

'Dead as a nit.'

'No motion, no breathing after he fell?'

'Not a whisper.'

Gently drank coffee. 'There may be a problem here,' he said. 'We shall come up against the medical report. At the moment, I am at a loss to see how we can deal with that.'

Lady Daphne also drank coffee. She said: 'Who was the lousy sawbones who wrote it?'

'A Dr Aldred.'

'So that's all right, then. Aldred shoots with us. Charles will have a word with him.'

'Regrettably, his report is now on record.'

'He can have second thoughts.'

Gently shook his head. 'In court, the defence may seek to minimize his findings, but the report is now evidence, and must go in.'

'Here!' Lady Daphne said. 'What's this about courts? It's a case for the local beaks to settle.'

'Unhappily, it cannot rest there. The report will take it to the Crown Courts.'

Lady Daphne's eyes were very mean. Her cup stayed poised above its saucer. She said:

'Now give it to me straight! What's in that bloody report of Aldred's?'

Gently drank coffee. He said: 'Concerning the cause of death, Aldred is positive. It was due to haemorrhaging occasioned by gunshot, with shock submitted as a secondary cause.'

'So what's wrong with that?'

'It means that death was delayed. That Stanton did not die instantaneously. That he would be seen to be still alive. That first-aid assistance may have saved his life.'

Her eyes were large. 'So he was bloody murdered?'

'I'm afraid that is the contention. Which of course makes it a matter for the Crown Courts. Though a good defence counsel may soften the impact.'

'Holy catfish.'

'Perhaps you will take it into consideration when you give me your statement, which is how we must proceed from now.' Gently drank. 'With any luck, we can arrange you a court appearance for tomorrow morning.'

'You bastard!'

'Shall we go?'

Her glare was homicidal. 'No. We won't!'

'You have changed your mind?'

Gently had risen and carried his cup to the tray. He poured more coffee and, after a hesitation, added a couple of drips of cream. Lady Daphne watched him with furious eyes. She said:

'You don't want to settle this business for us, do you?'

'On the contrary.'

'You know what I mean! So that it doesn't hit the Sunday papers. Look, you've got me. I'm willing. I've got a tale that could wind it all up. All you need do is to play ball and let one of our beaks put it to bed. So why don't you?'

Gently stirred sugar into his coffee. He said: 'You didn't· shoot Stanton, yet you are willing to pretend that you did. Of course, the question arises, why? What likely motive could you have?'

'I've told you my motive, you swine!'

Gently drank, then shook his head. 'Your daughter's motive was to protect her husband. Couldn't your motive be the same?'

'I'm going to complain about you!'

'A similar motive,' Gently said. 'Though not necessarily with the same object. Not Hugh Merton this time. Not even your daughter. So who else is in the picture, and may stand in grave risk?'

'You louse, and I trusted you!'

Gently shrugged. 'And at a risk that may suddenly have become graver?'

'I won't listen to you!'

'Which you may suspect. Or of which you may even have some knowledge?'

Lady Daphne merely eyed him. Gently took another swig from his cup. He said:

'Of course, this is pure conjecture, and your motive may have been what you say. But you will appreciate that your behaviour does suggest such a line of suspicion.'

'Just get out of here!' Lady Daphne snapped.

'Any comment I would welcome.'

'Out. Just get out!'

Gently put down his cup. And left the boudoir.

Outside he ran into Phipps, who appeared to have been loitering in the passage. The author surveyed him with a stare of irony, then placed a finger to his ear. He said:

'Don't accuse me of eaves dropping, but I caught that final insinuation of yours. And I understand you are bringing down an expert to confirm my ridiculous asseveration. Would this be true?'

'Have you some objection?'

'None. Except that my opinion was flouted in the first place. But stupidity I am inured to, even that of high-ranking officials.'

Gently paused to look him over. He said: 'And that opinion you don't wish to alter?'

'Not in the smallest, most insignificant detail. The Warren Lodge Constable has flown.'

'You wouldn't be seeking to direct suspicion?'

'What an idea,' Phipps said.

'Perhaps I should rephrase that. To redirect suspicion?'

'He tries,' Phipps said. 'How he tries.'

Gently said: 'On the Sunday. On your very lonely afternoon. After you had heard the gate close behind Stanton. Did you really hear the gate close again?'

Phipps's eyes hit his for an instant, then recoiled and drifted away. 'Read my statement,' he said. 'Read and learn. I don't see why I should be obliged to repeat it.'

'Did you?'

Phipps stroked his beard.

'I think you may have invented that,' Gently said. 'You heard Stanton leave, but nothing more. Your second thud kept you placed in the garden.'

Phipps stroked on.

'Where a witness says you weren't.'

Phipps gave him one long seething stare. Then he broke away, marched into the hall, and disappeared up the stairs. The concerned face of Sir Charles looked out of the study; but Gently went his way to join Calthorpe.

Calthorpe was standing by his car and surveying the house with a cogitative eye. He said:

'Not a sign of a break-in, sir. That place is sewn up like Fort Knox.'

141

'So it would be an inside job.'

'Yes, sir. Supposing there was a job done at all. But I've been standing here thinking, sir, and wondering if someone hasn't got a little game on.'

'Let's take a stroll.'

They went down the terrace, Gently filling his pipe as they went. At the bottom of the lawn they sat down on a bench, and Gently struck a light, and puffed.

'Now.'

'It's like this, sir. I've always had a question-mark against Mr Phipps. Motive, opportunity, he had them, and it was him who saw the deceased set out for the forest. So now we're dragging our feet over Merton, and Mr Phipps is getting uneasy. What's to be done? He pulls a trick like this, to try to get us looking in other directions.'

'Ye-es,' Gently conceded. 'But then it gets us looking very hard at Mr Phipps.'

'Could be he thinks it's worth it, sir, if it starts us chasing after someone else.'

'Brewster, for example?'

'Could be him, sir. But it's someone else who comes first to mind.'

'Mr Timothy.'

'I'd say he was the mark, sir. And we've always fancied him after Merton. And we're pretty certain he tampered with Gourbold, which was scarcely the act of an innocent man. But either would do, sir. He gets us thinking that one or other of them switched that painting, and the deceased was suspicious, and that's the motive. And Mr Phipps is Simon Pure.'

'Which . . . he might just be.'

Calthorpe hesitated. 'I can't think there's much doubt about the picture, sir! Sir Charles and his lady don't seem to have any, and they must know it better than anyone. No, sir, Mr Phipps is trying it on. And that has to be suspicious behaviour.'

142

Gently said: 'Seymour will be here after lunch.'

'And then we'll know it for a fact, sir.'

Gently said: 'Until then, we'd better leave it on the back burner. We do have three separate confessions from people who claim too have shot Laurence Stanton.'

'But . . . sir!'

'One has just been withdrawn. One we may discount. One we cannot.'

Calthorpe looked piqued. He stared back at the house for a few moments. Then at Gently. He said:

'I thought the old girl did the best job, sir!'

'It is Lady Daphne who has withdrawn.'

'That's a pity, sir. Hers might have stuck. It's the only one with the gun at a proper distance. And you could just see her jumping down off that horse, and getting into a tangle, and thinking she'd shot herself. I could have backed her.'

Gently sieved smoke. 'Lady Daphne is a considerable woman.'

'The daughter didn't have the facts right, sir. But I thought she put up a good show, too.'

'Cassandra Merton was merely seeking to protect her husband.'

'And he was trying to protect her.' Calthorpe stared at the lawn. 'But about Merton, sir. There's one thing we can't overlook. He couldn't easily have missed seeing Stanton lying there. Not if he came along like he said.'

'It would be unlikely. Though not impossible.'

'No, sir.' Calthorpe shook his head. 'And what he told us about the shooting doesn't square. It wasn't any accident that killed Stanton.'

'So. Another little talk with Merton.'

'Yes, sir. And forget Mr Phipps.'

'Let's go.'

They strolled back up the lawn to the car: a figure in the

143

porch stood watching them depart. Sweat-shirt and jeans, tousle-haired, furtive, Timothy Stanton stared after them with hostile eyes. Calthorpe glanced back as he swung the car.

'That's someone I'm not going to forget, sir,' he said.

10

Two scribbled sheets of statement-paper, waiting on the desk, showed that Merton had been busy since his return to the police station. Patiently Gently deciphered the sketchy handwriting, handing the first sheet to Calthorpe while he tackled the second. It was the confession he had made in the forest, with one or two hopeful emendations; now, following Laurence Stanton, he had caught sight of his wife, and had hidden until he saw her canter away. But substantially the confession was the same. At the end of his perusal, Calthorpe shook his head.

'Oh, dear me! We're not there yet, sir.'

'He may have done some more thinking since this was written.'

'Then he's got a bit still to do, sir, if he's going to walk out of here.'

'Fetch him in.'

Calthorpe fetched him. Merton entered the office with nervous step. He ventured a glance at the desk, at the statement, but kept his eyes firmly lowered. Calthorpe steered him to a chair. Merton sat. He clasped his hands on his knees, and stared at them. After a pause, Gently picked up the statement, then let it fall again on the desk. He said:

'I've read your statement, Merton. Now I have a simple question to put to you. Your wife and your mother-in-law were probably lying. The question is, were you?'

'I . . .' Merton fumbled for words.

'Well?'

'Cassie – she wasn't there. You've got to believe that.'

'Mrs Merton had certainly been at the spot.'

'Yes, I saw her, I put it down there. But – '

'You maintain you saw her?'

'Yes . . . and she saw me, stalking the Aussie! And she must have recognized me, for all she says. And that's why – ' His mouth quivered. 'But she'd gone. She rode off directly. It was all of ten minutes later when – '

'When you shot Stanton?'

Merton winced. 'When it all happened – like I've written down there! I didn't mean to shoot him, it's too absurd, I only wanted to get my gun back off him.'

'And that's the truth?'

'Yes. Cassie – '

'You wrestled with him for the gun?'

'Yes. Yes!'

'In the course of which you sent Stanton sprawling?'

'Yes – '

'In some way that made him turn his back to you?'

'I . . . yes.'

'And then, involuntarily, the gun swung into an aiming position, and, involuntarily, your finger hit the trigger, just as Stanton had reeled twelve feet away from you?'

Merton's blue eyes clung to Gently's.

'Well,' Gently said. 'Would you believe it?'

'I want a drink,' Merton blurted. 'I feel sick. I want a drink.'

'Then you agree you were lying?'

'I want a drink!' Merton croaked.

'Isn't it more likely that you were carrying the gun?'

A DC had accompanied Merton into the office, and Calthorpe sent him for a glass of water. Merton gulped it down greedily, the tumbler trembling in his grasp. His eye was on the two sheets of the statement, lying discarded where Gently had dropped them. He finished the last drop of water and handed the tumbler back to the DC. He said:

'You're not going to believe me now, are you?'

Gently said: 'Was it you who had the gun?'

Merton's hands clenched and unclenched. He blurted: 'Oh, bloody hell. It was my gun, wasn't it?'

'You took it with you.'

'Yes, I took it. So it's got nothing to do with Cassie, has it? I took it. I took it with me to the forest. Half the time I'm around there I take a gun.'

'Even on Sundays?'

'Yes, even on Sundays! The rabbits don't know what day it is. They're a pest, they're our enemy, and if you're going where they are you take a gun.'

'And that's why you took it? To shoot rabbits?'

'Or squirrels. Or magpies. Or whatever.'

'Or whatever?'

'Not the Aussie! How did I know I should find him there?'

Gently stared at him, said: 'Go on.'

Merton looked as though he might have wanted another drink. He said: 'So I took the bloody gun. But I never saw the Aussie till I was in the forest. Then I spotted him up the ride, going in the same direction as I was.'

'You went after him?'

'Yes, of course I went after him! But I wasn't trying to stalk him, nothing like that. I was just damned annoyed to find him there, because he might have scattered the rabbits before I could get in a shot.'

'You weren't stalking him, yet you hid from your wife?'

'Oh – that.' Merton studied his hands. 'Well, I don't know! That was instinctive. I didn't want her hanging on there, and I knew she would stay once she'd spotted me.'

Gently said: 'She would have scattered the rabbits.'

Merton's gaze jerked to his.

147

'Go on,' Gently said.

Merton stared once more at his hands. He said: 'I went after him. He was heading straight on into the dell. I called after him, told him to wait, and he waited there till I came up.'

'He waited in the dell?'

'In the ride. I wanted to keep him out of the dell. That's where you go to get your shot, but there wouldn't have been one if he'd gone in there.'

'But weren't the rabbits already dispersed by your wife?'

'No – she'd gone! They'd be creeping back. In fact, I could see some scuts bobbing about there, one or two. He'd only to keep clear.'

'Go on,' Gently said.

'Yes, well. So I told him what I wanted to do. But he was in a temper – to do with Timothy, no doubt – and said he would go where he damned well pleased.'

'And then there was this struggle?' Gently touched the statement.

'No! You know it couldn't have been like that.'

'So, how was it?'

'He – he carried on. Into the dell. Just to spoil it for me.' Merton's hands were grappling. 'For a moment I stood there. I couldn't believe he would be so mean. Then I started to go in after him, and . . . I tripped. And that was it.'

'You . . . tripped.'

'On a bramble or something! I don't know what it was.'

'And the gun discharged?'

'Yes.'

'At . . . a range of twelve feet?'

'Yes – if you say so!' Merton wrung his hands. 'It happened so quickly. We both of us went down. I guessed I must have hit him, but I didn't think for one moment that it was so serious. But when I scrambled up he didn't move, just lay there, sprawled on his face. Then I saw where it had got him, saw the blood. And I knew.'

'He was dead.'

'Yes. Dead. And I don't care what you say.'

'You are not impressed by the medical opinion.'

'I was there. I saw it. The Aussie was dead.'

Gently nodded gravely. 'Go on.'

Merton didn't catch his eye. He said: 'You know the rest. It's what's down there, in my statement. People knew I had it in for him, then there was telling Sir Charles and all the rest of it. So I panicked. I raced back to the house and managed to drop the gun off in the gun-room, then I made myself scarce till I saw people going in for tea.'

'While, back in the forest, Laurence Stanton was dying.'

'No. I swear he was dead.'

'And after you had wiped your fingerprints from the gun.'

'I – well, I didn't want to take any chances, did I?'

'Clearly.'

Merton hesitated. 'So now you know everything,' he said. 'A clean breast, and I'm only sorry I didn't have the sense to tell you before. But that's what happened. I'm the one responsible. You can just forget what Cassie told you. So you can tear up that silly statement, and I'll write you the one I should have given in the first place.'

'A fresh statement.'

'Yes. The truth.'

Gently said: 'Then let me tell you what will follow. When your statement is written I shall charge you with the murder of Laurence Stanton, when you will be remanded to the gaol at Abbotsham and, in the morning, appear before a magistrate.'

'I'll . . . what?'

For an instant the blue eyes stared complete unbelief at Gently. Then Merton sprang up from his chair. The DC assisted him to sit again.

'But you can't do that!'

'Just listen.'

The freckles were prominent against the pallor of Merton's face. He was trembling, his eyes in a stare; his breath came fast through gaping lips.

'But – you can't. I didn't murder him!'

'What you have told us doesn't stand up.'

'It was an accident!'

'There is no way it could have been. If you write that statement, I must charge you. And if you do not, I must still remind you that your confession was made before witnesses.'

'Oh, my God. I'm going to be sick.'

'Fetch Mr Merton another glass of water.'

The DC fetched it. Merton gulped. The sweat was standing out on his forehead. In his eyes the unbelief lingered, and now he couldn't drag them away from Gently's.

'But I didn't . . .'

'Listen, Merton. We'll try to get a little closer to the truth. If you did take that gun with you, then it wasn't to shoot rabbits. Not on a Sunday. You made it quite plain that it was an etiquette you approved of.'

'But rabbits . . .'

Gently shook his head. 'Nor, at the dell, were there rabbits to shoot at. Your wife had scattered them. So there was no reason for you to ask Stanton to stay out of the dell.'

Merton just breathed harder.

Gently said: 'But the main objection to your tale is this. Your behaviour in the ride when you caught sight of your wife. You didn't wave, didn't hasten to meet her. By your own account, you hid. You didn't want her to see you, and why would that be, if your only object there was to shoot rabbits?'

Merton opened his mouth, but got no further.

Gently said: 'Then, later, the wiping of the gun will scarcely pass as an act of innocence. And we are given only

150

a flat contradiction of the incontrovertible medical evidence.' He paused. 'So what does it add up to? What would a jury make of it in court?'

Merton was swaying on the chair. 'But ... but I'm innocent. I am!'

Slowly, Gently shook his head. 'Not on the account that you've just given us.'

'It was only the rabbits ...'

'No.'

'You've got to believe me. You must.'

Gently said: 'It won't work, Merton.'

'Yes!'

'On that tale, I shall have to charge you. It might be best if you simply came clean, and pleaded guilty. It will save you much harassment.'

'But ...!'

The wretched forest-conservator dragged his gaze from Gently, turned it imploringly to Calthorpe. But met only a fascinated stare.

'Well?'

'It's – it's – '

'Yes?'

'It's – all a lie,' Merton croaked. 'All of it – all I've said. I never had the gun. I was nowhere near there.'

'Do you expect us to believe that now?'

'I was nowhere near – I did what I told you! Section 10. The pine-tip moths. I heard the gun go off when I was there.'

'And – returned by the dell?'

'I didn't see him.'

'He was still alive, Merton.'

'No! If he was alive, I didn't see him. I was in a hurry to get back to tea.'

'You could scarcely have missed him.'

'I tell you I did.'

'You are not claiming complete innocence?'

151

'Yes – oh yes!'

Gently pondered on the man who sat crouched and swaying across the desk. He said:

'So let us see where that gets us. Given your innocence of all that happened. There can be no question that Mrs Merton was at the spot at the time when Laurence Stanton arrived there.'

'Not Cassie . . . no. Please!'

'At the spot,' Gently said. 'And from Mrs Merton we also have a confession. If we are to accept the hypothesis of your innocence, then it follows we must take a closer look at Mrs Merton.'

'You wouldn't. You can't.'

'That must be the next step.'

'But she only said all that because of me!'

Gently held his stare. 'That remains to be determined. Mrs Merton had opportunity and also motive, and assuming your innocence we shall be obliged to consider her.'

'You can't – no!'

Gently shrugged. 'Always assuming your innocence,' he said.

'She didn't do it.'

'But with that assumption?'

'Oh, my God, my God!' Merton cried.

And then they lost him. For a brief instant his wild eyes swam before Gently's; his mouth opened. But before he could speak, he lurched, and collapsed out of the chair.

Calthorpe and the DC ran to catch him, and sought to prop him up again. But Merton was out in a dead faint. In the end, they carried him to a bench in reception.

Calthorpe sent out for a nip of brandy, and before long the shocked conservator was sitting up and looking less pale. But he'd had enough; he remained stubbornly mute and inaccessible to further questioning. They left him with the

DC. In the office, the two sheets of statement-paper still lay on the desk. After a pause, Gently picked them up, tore them across and dropped them into the waste-bin. Calthorpe said:

'So do we charge him, sir?'

Gently shook his head. 'No.'

'But . . . there's a case there.'

'Almost a case.'

'I'd say we could win it, sir,' Calthorpe said.

'I wonder.' Gently filled his pipe, lit it, drew till it flavoured. He said: 'The problem is, we could still be dealing with an innocent man.'

'But it all fits, sir, the way he told it. No jury is going to give him a chance. Him ducking out of sight when he saw his wife will be the clincher, you were right there.'

'Don't forget he's gone back to square one.'

'And that's a point for us, sir, the way I see it. He thought his opening up was going to get him off, and then he tried to change his tune when he found it wouldn't.'

'We don't have his statement.'

'But we've got him on the run, sir. One more session, and he could come clean.'

Gently puffed broodingly. He said: 'Taken on its own, we'd be near to a case! But it isn't on its own. There's confusion in the background. And most immediate to Merton, the situation of his wife.'

Calthorpe was frowning. 'You can't mean that, sir – not that you believe what she was giving us?'

'But she was there, which puts pressure on Merton. And that isn't the only business we have to allow for.'

'You mean this picture lark?'

Gently nodded.

'And – Mr Timothy?'

'We can't ignore him.'

Calthorpe thought about it. 'I don't know,' he said. 'I can't see any of that holding us up for long. So Mr Timothy

153

was in the running, but like the man said, would he have the nerve? I'd like to do him for tampering with Gourbold, but I can't see him going after Stanton with a gun. Then Mr Phipps and his games – no, I can't see that horse running. And Mrs Merton, she did us a favour. So it keeps adding up to chummie, sir.'

Gently puffed. 'Almost.'

'All the way is my opinion, sir.'

Gently said: 'Oddly enough, at last, I got the impression that Merton was trying to tell us the truth.'

'You mean – square one, sir?'

'Square one.'

Calthorpe considered, then shook his head. 'He was trying all right, sir, but I can't say he impressed me.'

'Just his last throw.'

'Yes, sir. And he should have seen the bloke. No, unless something new turns up, I'm keeping my money where it is.'

'Perhaps you are right.' Gently took more puffs. 'Meanwhile, we have Seymour arriving on the two-thirty from town.'

'The Fraud Squad man, sir?'

Gently nodded. 'Have a car laid on at the station.'

'And – Merton, sir?'

Gently made a face. 'Give him some lunch, and keep him supplied with statement-paper. And otherwise treat him like a human being.'

'Right you are,' Calthorpe said. 'I get the message.'

Gently rang Gabrielle, then made his way down to The Cross Keys. At once he was aware of a forlorn figure lounging in a retired corner of the bar. Gently ignored him, ordered a pint and a plate of ham salad. While the barmaid was fetching the latter, the landlord came across. He nodded to the figure.

'Have you seen him?'

'I've seen him,' Gently said.

'Come in here looking for young Gourbold. Only young Gourbold wasn't around.' The landlord looked sly. 'What's he done?'

Gently merely shrugged and drank his beer.

'Well, we haven't seen a hair of him since yesterday,' the landlord said. 'Though I can't say I'm grieving very much about that.'

Gently's salad arrived. He added condiments and carried it to a table at some distance from the figure in the corner. The eyes of the latter followed him angrily, but Gently continued in his oblivion. He ate and drank, and regarded the picture, spared an occasional glance for the customers; but his eye never strayed to the corner where Timothy Stanton sat before an empty glass.

'What's for sweet?'

'Try the cheesecake, squire. You won't have any quarrels with that.'

The landlord had a keen eye on the little drama that was enacting.

'Cream or ice-cream?'

'Both.'

The landlord winked as he handed it over.

'Coffee, squire?'

'Coffee.'

'The girl will bring it over to you.'

The cheesecake was worth its recommendation, and Gently ate it without haste. Then he dallied over the coffee, floating in the cream with his spoon. But it was not until he pushed his cup away and began to fill his pipe that Timothy Stanton rose to his feet and made his way to Gently's table. Then he stood glowering down at Gently, hands dug deep in the pockets of his jeans.

'Take a seat,' Gently said.

'Oh, we're being so clever!' Timothy Stanton said. 'I'm a

155

naughty boy, aren't I, and that's the way you're going to treat me.'

'Have you been naughty?' Gently said.

'Oh yes. Because I'm not responsible for you know what. So we've been wasting our valuable time, haven't we, when we should have been concentrating on dear Hugh.'

'I try not to waste my time,' Gently said.

'Don't tell me he's finally confessed,' Timothy Stanton said. 'You can't have been as clever as all that. Has he confessed? Is Hugh in the bag?'

'Why don't you sit down?' Gently said.

'Yes, why don't I?' Timothy Stanton said. 'Perhaps he will even buy me a drink. While he tries to turn me inside out.'

Gently didn't buy him a drink, but Timothy Stanton sat clumsily down. He did so with his back to the bar, where the landlord was watching all with a gleeful eye. He fixed a sneering gaze on Gently . . . or was there something else in that distasteful leer? He said:

'So dear Hugh hasn't been such a walk-over, and the Constabulary eye is still lifting. Well, well. But if you don't fancy him, I hear my sister is telling a good tale. Won't she do?'

Gently said nothing.

'I'd look at her twice,' Timothy Stanton said. 'She's almost breaking her fair neck to put herself in your clutches. If you don't like her story, just put her straight. She'll be happy to toe the line. And nobody's going to throw the book at Cassie over a little carelessness with a gun.'

Gently said nothing.

'Not Cassie either,' Timothy Stanton said. 'Could the Man still be having a soft spot for me? Naughty Timothy? Who wasn't playing tapes when Emma Spinks went tripping by? Oh, I've had it out with Emma. But I wouldn't bank on her as a witness. I've got Dennys on my side,

156

remember, unless the rotten so-and-so lets me down. What do you say? Shall I confess too?'

Gently said: 'Do you wish to?'

'Oh, dear me, why not?' Timothy Stanton said. 'It seems to be becoming a family tradition.'

'So what did you trip over,' Gently said. 'A rabbit?'

'I didn't trip,' Timothy Stanton said. 'When I shot the Aussie I meant it. Isn't that what the Man wants to hear?'

'Intentionally, you shot your stepbrother?'

'All the way down the line,' Timothy Stanton said. 'Except, oh dear, I've just remembered, I was somewhere entirely different at the time. Sad but true – isn't it a shame? Now, are you going to buy me a drink?'

Gently didn't buy him a drink. He said: 'I've been studying that picture of yours over there.'

'My picture?' Timothy Stanton said.

'Your picture. It seems a little different from the ones I looked at on the houseboat.'

Timothy Stanton was silent for a moment. Then he sneered: 'The bucolic taste.'

'Bucolic . . . ?'

'What one sells to publicans. You wouldn't expect them to be tempted by caviar, would you?'

'Yet, a pleasant picture.'

'Oh, your humble servant.'

'Not so far removed from the masters,' Gently said.

Timothy Stanton said nothing.

'From Crome, from Wilson,' Gently said. 'From Morland. Or possibly Constable.'

Timothy Stanton said nothing.

'Of course,' Gently said, 'you've been brought up, you live in that atmosphere. In daily association with the masters. The likes of Gainsborough and Turner. And Constable. You would clearly have taken lessons from the best.'

'I paint in my own way!' Timothy Stanton spat.

Gently nodded. 'Yet the influence shows through. Even

157

in those pictures displayed in the houseboat. In those flashes of realism among the chaos.'

'Who says it's chaos?'

Gently bowed his head. 'What, to a layman like me, appears chaos. You may call it by a different name. It may represent the turmoil of a repressed spirit.'

'Oh, sneer, sneer!' Timothy Stanton hissed.

'A spirit repressed by unlucky circumstance. By the lack of support that might release it. By the lack of belief. By the lack of money.'

'You sneering devil!' Timothy Stanton snarled. 'You know nothing. You're a lout, a Philistine. You're worse than him.' He jerked a thumb at the landlord. 'Who gave you the right to talk of these things?'

Gently shrugged. 'They're out of my province. That's why I'm calling in an expert.'

'Damn your expert. And I'll tell you something. Our mighty Mr Phipps isn't waiting for his opinion.'

'Mr Phipps . . .?'

'Mr Phipps. He's packed his bags and left for town.'

'Mr Phipps has left?'

'Skedaddled. Gone. Maybe he remembered an urgent appointment.'

Gently said: 'He left by car?'

'Yes, as far as the station,' Timothy Stanton sneered. 'And it wasn't in the Bentley either. Dear Emma drove him down in her Metro.'

Gently checked his watch; he rose. To the landlord he said: 'May I use your phone?'

Timothy Stanton sat glaring for a while, then he, too, rose; and slunk out of the bar.

158

11

The London train was signalled as Gently left The Cross
Keys and hastened down the street, but it was still a distant
rumble when he strode through the booking-hall and on to
the platform. Phipps was the solitary passenger waiting
there. Beside him stood a large suitcase and a couple of
bags. He turned abruptly as Gently appeared and met the
detective with a flat stare. He said:

'Can it be that I have forgotten something?'

For reply, Gently picked up the bags and suitcase. He
said: 'I must ask you to accompany me, Mr Phipps. You will
not be taking the train to town.'

'Exactly what do you mean?'

'That you must remain here. Your presence is required in
the investigation. In addition, I must also ask you to submit
to an examination of your luggage.'

'You are joking, of course.'

'I am not joking.'

'Then I must tell you I completely and utterly refuse.'

'In that case, I shall be obliged to arrest you.'

'In that case, you will proceed at your peril.'

At which point the train rumbled in, and Calthorpe and
Bodney arrived, panting, on the platform. For an instant, it
looked as though Phipps might make an attempt to board
the train, and Bodney hastened to place himself between
them. He received a withering glance from Phipps, who
then drew himself tall, and stared icily at Gently.

'Very well, then. If I am under compulsion.'

'That's right, sir,' Calthorpe panted. 'We don't want any trouble, sir.'

'But I reserve the right to make an official complaint.'

'Of course, sir. But if you'll just come along with us, now.'

Gently handed the baggage to Bodney, and led the way to the station waiting-room. There, under the blazing eye of its owner, the catches were snapped on the big suitcase. Two suits, carefully folded, emerged, and several flat-files stuffed with typescript; then there was another of Phipps's smartly cut blazers, and a bunch of expensive silk ties. But of liberated paintings there was no sign. The bags contained merely underwear, toiletry and shoes. Phipps's stare now had a glint of triumph.

'And for this I have been compelled to miss my train?'

Gently said: 'I think it must have occurred to you that we cannot permit anyone concerned to leave Breckford.'

'Indeed? Then I am regarded as a fugitive?'

'For the moment, your presence is required at the Lodge.'

'I am under suspicion?'

Gently said: 'I think you are aware of your situation.'

'My situation – oh yes!' Phipps drew himself tall again. 'I have given a troublesome opinion about a painting, which now I am to be asked to see controverted. And I spend a quiet afternoon with the Sunday reviews, an act which renders my presence quite indispensable. Is there more?'

Gently merely stared. Phipps tried to stare him down, but failed. Calthorpe said:

'If you'll just take it easy, sir, we'll give you a ride back to the Lodge in a few minutes.'

'And if I don't wish to go there?'

'Just take it easy, sir. That's the best advice I can give you.'

Phipps didn't take it easy: he threw himself down on a

bench and sat fuming. Meanwhile the signal for the down-line had gone, and shortly the train bearing Seymour drew in at the other platform. Bodney was sent across to collect him. The Fraud Squad man appeared, carrying a brief-case. About to enter the waiting-room, his eye fell on Phipps, and he paused, then beckoned to Gently. Gently joined him. Seymour said:

'That laddie in there – is he part of the comedy?'

'Do you know him?'

'Dear me, yes! I've had several chats with Lofty Leslie.'

'Chats about what?'

'Oh, this and that. But rather more about that. He was writing a book on a certain subject, for which he consulted me. Now you guess what.'

Gently said: 'On fakes?'

'Better still. On marketing fakes.'

'Marketing them!'

'Uhuh,' Seymour grinned. 'And you haven't heard the half of it, yet. There's a darling rumour going around about a foot-loose Constable soon to hit the market, while a certain American has booked into the Hilton who sets red lights flashing wherever he goes. Interesting, eh?'

'Very interesting.'

'And Lofty Leslie right on the spot. Could it have been him who potted the Australian?'

'He's in the running.'

'Well, well,' Seymour said.

Gently said: 'What doesn't quite fit is Phipps alleging the picture to be a fake.'

'Ah,' Seymour said. 'He's paving the way. Planning a switch at a later date. He makes a hoo-hah, the picture is checked out, then, when the fuss dies away, the switch. That way everyone is conditioned to accept the switcheroo as real.'

'Wouldn't he do better to stay quiet about it?'

'You might think so, I might think so. But it's a trick that's been played before, and I wouldn't put it past Lofty Les. No, in a way I'm wasting my time. I'd say the switch hadn't happened yet. But then, if we can tie this in with your job, perhaps it will never happen at all.'

Gently shrugged. 'So let's get you to the painting!'

'My pleasure,' Seymour said. 'I'm happy with Constables. I like a well-made Turner too, but I wish the villains would stay away from Goghy.'

Sir Charles was waiting for them on the steps, and he seemed a little embarrassed at seeing Phipps arrive with them. But after a moment's hesitation he came forward and clasped the author's hand.

'So you've changed your mind, Leslie! Well, I have to admit that I'm relieved. This is a very foolish business, and the sooner it's forgotten the better.'

'I', Phipps said, 'have not changed my mind. My appearance here has been compelled.'

'Compelled? You mean – ?'

'Under pain of arrest. I should now be on the London train.'

Sir Charles stared and shook his head, but then deftly dropped the subject. He greeted Seymour with a firm handshake, and hastened the party into the house. In the gallery the lights were switched on. There, Lady Daphne and the others had collected. Brewster had his manilla envelope with him; he pulled a face when he caught sight of Phipps. Cassandra Merton stared eagerly at Gently, but kept her station beside her mother. Emma Spinks hovered on call. Timothy Stanton alone was missing. Sir Charles marched Seymour up to the Constable.

'There, officer,' he said. 'That's the bone of contention. In my view it is the picture I bought twenty years ago, but the question has arisen and you must decide. Please take all the time you need. A definitive opinion is what we require.'

162

Seymour viewed the painting with squinting eyes. 'Yes,' he said. 'Very nice. Very nice. The old boy at his sweetest. You couldn't ask for better than that.'

'You incline to the view that it is genuine?'

Seymour hissed through his teeth and rocked his shoulders.

'Of course it is,' Lady Daphne said, with a fierce eye on Phipps. 'Anything else is absurd. A fool could tell you it's the same painting.'

Phipps returned her stare with interest. He was standing aside, attended by Bodney. Brewster was fiddling with his envelope, and giving the author little sly glances.

Seymour moved closer to the painting. 'Yes, nice, very nice,' he said. He trailed a thumb-nail across one corner, then repeated the action higher up. 'Been cleaned lately?'

'Two months ago,' Sir Charles said. 'I borrowed the team from the Nat. I believe in the best.'

'They're the best,' Seymour said. 'Hmn. I think we'll have him down, if we may.'

'Whatever you require.'

Seymour unhooked the painting and took it across to the nearest bench. After scanning the face of it for some moments he reversed it, and studied the back. His fingers ran over the canvas, the panel-pins, the frame, then repeated these motions. He regarded the picture with an affectionate expression.

'Nice, nice. Now I think we'll have him out.'

'You mean – out of the frame?' Sir Charles frowned.

'Just a quick look-see,' Seymour said.

From his brief-case he took a pair of grips, and with them began removing the pins. Sir Charles stood by with a flinching scowl, the others with fascinated stares. One by one the pins came out, till finally there were no more. Then, with great delicacy, Seymour nudged the painting from the frame. He ran his fingers along the edges.

'Lovely . . . lovely. A lovely job.'

163

'I take it you are satisfied?' Sir Charles said.

'Half a mo',' Seymour said. 'I want you to see this for yourself.'

From his pocket he dug out a penknife, and clicked open the blade. Then, before a scandalized Sir Charles could intervene, he had scraped the blade firmly along one edge of the painting.

'Oh, my lord! What have you done?' Sir Charles exclaimed.

'Just removed some Winsor and Newton.'

'Some . . . what?'

Seymour pointed to the scrape. It showed hard and brown amongst the lighter sky-colouring.

'Isn't it lovely?' Seymour said. 'I wonder how your Mr Phipps knew?'

'You . . . you are saying?'

'It's a gorgeous fake. And it seems to have kidded all of you except one.'

'A fake . . . '

Still Sir Charles didn't seem able to take it in. He stared at Seymour, stared at the picture, at the tell-tale weal of old paint among the new.

'But it's the picture Sotheby's sold me! Are you telling me I bought a pup? That all these years . . . ?'

Seymour shook his head. 'This one hasn't been painted that long.'

'Then . . . what?'

'I'm afraid you've been robbed. And what I want now is to get to a phone. One of the top buyers of liberated paintings, by a strange coincidence, has just hit town.'

'A buyer? Then this was all planned?'

'From A to Zee. And points beyond.'

Emma Spinks showed Seymour to a phone, and the stunned Sir Charles sat down on a bench. Lady Daphne, for once nonplussed, could only stare at the demoted picture. Cassandra Merton ran to her father. Brewster was getting out his photograph. Phipps, after a brief hesitation, took a few steps closer to the others. He said:

'After all the insinuations, may it perhaps be allowed that I do know my business?'

'Shut up, Leslie,' Lady Daphne snapped. 'If you start crowing I shall hit you.'

'As you wish,' Phipps sneered. 'But it did happen to be me who spotted the fake. And had I been paid the attention I deserved, some hours of valuable time might have been saved. Because the switch was made last night. This morning, the original may still have been on the premises. While now it is probably on its way to the buyer we have been told of.'

'I shall hit you,' Lady Daphne snapped.

'And what about this photograph, Les,' Brewster put in. 'It was taken on Sunday, and it shows that painting. So how could the switch have been made last night?'

'If it was taken on Sunday, it is not of this painting.'

'But damn it, Les, you can see it is!'

'Or, alternatively,' Phipps said, 'if it is of this painting, then it was not taken on Sunday.'

Brewster wasn't grinning now. 'And what exactly do you mean by that?'

'Oh, pay no attention to him!' Lady Daphne said. 'Leslie has been a mistake all along. And I notice he has a policeman attached to him, which suggests he might do well to pipe down.'

Sir Charles uttered a deep groan.

'Oh, Daddy, Daddy!' Cassandra Merton murmured.

Sir Charles shook, kept shaking, his bowed head. He said: 'What I'm thinking just cannot be! It's Laurence. He was asking about the picture. He wanted me to tell him how much it was worth.'

'Oh, Daddy, don't!'

'Yes . . . Laurence. He had been around, met all sorts of people. And I didn't really know him, though he was my son. But he was interested in the picture.'

Lady Daphne stared at him but said nothing.

'And out of the blue he arrives here,' Sir Charles said. 'I have to think it. I may be wronging him, but somehow I can't rid myself of the connection.'

'Daddy, it's nonsense!' Cassandra Merton pleaded.

But Sir Charles continued shaking his head.

Calthorpe said to Gently: 'I don't know about you, sir, but I reckon that search should still go ahead. If there's a chance that the picture's still here, we don't want to miss a trick.'

Sir Charles had heard him: his head jerked up. He said: 'Yes – a search. Begin at once, officer!'

'Oh, hang on, Charles!' Lady Daphne said. 'We don't want the place turned over just like that.'

'But there's a chance that it's here.'

'A pretty slim one. It's odds on that the picture is long gone.'

'You can search my quarters,' Brewster said. 'As long as you turn over Les's too.'

Sir Charles closed his eyes. 'Laurence's room. Nobody has been in there since Sunday.'

'Oh, Charles!'

'Search it. Search it! I have to know where we stand.'

'You're being ridiculous.'

'I can't help it. I want Laurence's room searched first of all.'

Calthorpe looked at Gently: Gently nodded. Calthorpe spoke a word to Bodney.

'Call Emma,' Sir Charles said. 'She'll show you where. And get on with the rest of the house straight afterwards.'

Calthorpe left; Bodney stayed beside Phipps. A moment later, Seymour returned. He looked at Phipps. He said:

'That's put the stopper on, back in town. There'll be a

certain American booking his flight – didn't his name come up in our little conversations?'

Calthorpe reported in person that Laurence Stanton's room was clean, and by then his troops had arrived and a general search of the Lodge commenced. Phipps had failed to respond to Seymour's insinuations; he sat on a bench, looking supremely bored. Seymour had borrowed Brewster's photograph and was matching it point by point with the fake Constable, and shortly Sir Charles, Lady Daphne and Cassandra Merton retired up the gallery for a family consultation. Gently drifted out of the gallery. In the hall he met Emma Spinks. She had two dog-leads in her hand; she gave Gently a nervous glance. She said:

'I'm not wanted – am I?'

'You're not wanted,' Gently said.

'You see, it's my time to walk the dogs. Though with everything that's going on . . .'

Gently shrugged. He said: 'Have you seen Timothy Stanton since lunch?'

'Oh – yes!' Emma Spinks coloured. 'He called in at the house. But he isn't here now.'

'So where would I find him?'

'Well . . . at the houseboat. He's usually there if he isn't here.' She hesitated, then stammered: 'Do you especially want Timothy, then?'

'I wish to speak to him.'

'Yes . . . of course! Well, I'd better collect the dogs.'

She hurried away. Gently let her go. He took the path that led to the houseboat. From a distance he could hear the sound of Timothy Stanton's tape-player; it was playing Benjamin Britten's War Requiem. The houseboat appeared deserted, but as Gently approached Timothy Stanton emerged from the cabin. He stood watching with wary eyes

167

as Gently stepped aboard and climbed down into the well. He said:

'What do you want?'

Gently said: 'Our conversation at The Cross Keys was interrupted. Also, you may care to know that the status of the Warren Lodge Constable has been confirmed.'

'It's been . . . what?'

'Confirmed,' Gently said. 'Our expert has given us a definitive opinion. If you had waited at the house you would have heard it. I believe he admired the picture very much.'

'But what – what – ?' This time, it was Timothy Stanton who switched off the tape-player. 'Just what are you trying to tell me – why can't you say what you mean!'

'I thought I was making it clear,' Gently said. 'The workmanship appealed to him highly.'

'But what did he say?'

'What should he say? As a fake, he'd rarely seen a better.'

'As . . . a fake.'

'A talented fake. You may remember how it deceived your father.'

'Then, if it's a fake – '

Gently nodded. 'Certain steps are, of course, being taken.'

Timothy Stanton slumped on a wicker chair, his eyes small under the bush of hair. Gently switched on the tape-player again, but turned the volume down low. He said:

'Have you anything to say?'

'Yes, you bastard! It wasn't me.'

Gently said: 'Access, skill, privacy. Who else can there be who enjoys these advantages?'

'But you can't prove it.'

'And the switch,' Gently said. 'Of necessity, that was an inside job. So many circumstances pointing one way. Simple proof would seem almost superfluous.'

'But you can't. You can't prove it.'

'Simple proof,' Gently said. He moved across to the easel, the palette, the brushes; the tubes of paint that littered the tray of the easel. He picked up one of the latter, let it fall again. 'Simple proof.'

'But it isn't – it proves nothing.'

'We shall have it analysed,' Gently said.

'But it's the paint that everyone uses!'

'There will be variations in different batches.'

'I don't care. It isn't proof. All you're doing is trying to trap me. Well, it didn't work before, and it damn well isn't going to now. So – so – get off my boat!'

Gently didn't get off his boat. Instead he began collecting together the tubes of paint and repacking them in their colour-box. To this he added the collection of brushes and, after a moment's thought, the paint-scabbed palette and a bottle of varnish. He said:

'One circumstance is lacking! You would need to find a buyer for the original. The faking, yes, and the switching. But finding buyers is in a separate league. For that, in what direction should we be looking?'

'Get off my boat!' Timothy Stanton hissed. 'This is your idea, your try-on. If you want to invent things, I can't stop you.'

'I'm afraid it follows,' Gently said. 'You couldn't have worked this trick on your own. You would need a confederate, an inside man, one who had contacts and knew the market.' He paused. 'Say, a well-travelled man. A man who had knocked around the world?'

'You're mad,' Timothy Stanton hissed. 'Quite mad.'

Gently stared at him, then slowly nodded. 'Yes,' he said. 'It doesn't fit, does it? Your stepbrother had a different role to play. What we're looking for is an expert in paintings, in the world of collectors, the paintings market. And don't we have one here?'

'You're mad. Mad.'

'Ready to hand,' Gently said.

169

'You're inventing it. Inventing everything. And you can't prove a bloody thing.'

'A faker. An agent.'

'I tell you, you're mad!'

'Then we come to Sunday,' Gently said.

Timothy Stanton jerked away from him, crouching, his eyes big. Gently didn't look at Timothy Stanton. He looked at the easel. He said:

'Your stepbrother was already suspicious. He had seen the photographer making free with the Constable. That wasn't the reason why he followed you down here. But when he got here, what did he see?'

'He didn't see anything!'

'I think he did. I think it is the reason he is dead now.'

'You're mad – crazy!'

Gently said: 'In the balance was five million pounds.' He turned from the easel to the row of lockers that ran down the length of the well. He said: 'The house is being searched, of course, in case the picture is still on the premises. But where would be a more likely place to conceal a five-million-pound painting?'

'You – you get off my boat!'

Gently shook his head and began opening the lockers.

'You can't do that – you need a warrant!'

'Then that's a risk I shall have to take.'

'Oh, you brute, you swine!'

For an instant it seemed likely that Timothy Stanton would hurl himself at Gently; the next, he had sprung ashore and was racing away up the bank. Gently checked an impulse to call after him. Timothy Stanton wasn't heading towards the house, but had taken the path to the Round Garden. Gently watched him go, shrugged, and returned to the lockers.

He searched the lockers in the well, and then the lockers in the cabins; the built-in wardrobes, the toilet, the galley and the forepeak. He found a number of Timothy Stanton's paintings, some of them attempts at the classic style, and one that might have been a study for the fake; but the Constable he did not find. He lit his pipe, and considered the houseboat. He tested the panelling that lined the interior, tapped the planking of the double roof, raised the bunk-boards in the cabins. The bilges alone remained. They seemed an unlikely prospect for a property of such worth and vulnerability; nevertheless, one by one, Gently lifted the floor-boards in the cabins and the well. And there finally, in the bilge of the latter, half-submerged in cloudy water, he came upon a package wrapped in bin-bags and sealed with a wealth of sticky tape. He let the water drain from it. He cut the tape. He removed each bin-bag with delicate care. And the canvas came out dry and unharmed: he was looking at John Constable's *Grange Farm, Woolpit*. He replaced it in one of the bin-bags; and set off for the house with five million pounds tucked underneath his arm.

'Where is Phipps?'

'Gone up to his room, sir. But I have left a man outside.'

He met Calthorpe at the cars, where the local man had been calling in for extra assistance. Gently rested his package on the roof of the car. He said:

'Did Timothy Stanton pass this way?'

'No, sir. I haven't seen him lately.'

'When you do see him, grab him.'

'Grab him, sir . . .?'

'Place him under arrest. I'm afraid that Timothy Stanton is our man. And send a DC down to the houseboat to pick up some evidence waiting there.'

'Some evidence?'

'And call off the search. Timothy Stanton had the picture hidden on the houseboat.'

He filled Calthorpe in. Calthorpe listened with widening eyes. When he realized what the package contained, he edged back from it, almost as though he thought it might bite him. He said:

'Then all this time Merton has been telling the truth, sir?'

'It would seem so. At least, in the case of his original statement.'

'And it's Mr Timothy who's behind all of it?'

'Mr Timothy. And one other.'

'But it must have been him, sir, with the gun. I never could see Mr Phipps doing that!'

Gently shook his head. 'Probably not. He just heard the second thud of the gate.'

'While Mr Timothy . . .' Calthorpe's eyes were seeing it. 'He'd had a beating into the bargain, sir. And on top his stepbrother had spotted his little game. I reckon the Aussie was dead when he left that houseboat.'

'Guns being so available.'

'Right, sir. Mr Timothy would have been round here like a flash. And Mrs Merton saw him, going after his step-brother, which at first she was half-way to telling us. It all fits in.'

Gently said: 'Except Phipps.'

'Lost his nerve, sir,' Calthorpe said. 'He wanted out, so he blew the whistle. He's hoping there's no way we can tie him in.'

Gently said: 'You may be right. And meanwhile, we have to inform the family.'

'Yes, sir,' Calthorpe said. 'And it won't be funny. Though I'm not sure that some of them aren't expecting it.'

They were interrupted by the appearance of Emma Spinks behind a pair of straining spaniels: an Emma Spinks with a more-than-usual expression of alarm on her perspiring face. She said:

'What's wrong with Timothy? He just rushed past me without a word, and looking as though he'd seen a ghost. What have you been doing to him?'

Gently said: 'In which direction was he going, Miss Spinks?'

'Towards the forest. But there's something wrong! Oughtn't someone to go after him?'

12

Calthorpe got on his radio again: soon, cars would be patrolling the forest roads; then he hastened back to the house with Gently, to call off and redeploy his men. In the gallery Seymour sat alone, drinking coffee and devouring cream cakes. He winked at Gently. He said:

'I do like these trips in the country!'

'Just check this over, will you?'

Gently laid his package on the bench. Seymour eyed it, eyed Gently, then put down his cup and unwrapped the package. He let the bin-bags fall to the floor.

'Holy Keating . . .! Where did you find it?'

'Half-submerged in the bilge of a houseboat. So you'd better check that it's OK.'

'In a sodding houseboat! Whose?'

'The boat is occupied by Timothy Stanton.'

'The son who paints?'

Gently nodded.

'Glory be,' Seymour said.

He stood the canvas beside the fake. The difference was subtle, but quite distinct. The glow, the luminosity was largely lost in the painstaking copy. For such as Phipps, it might have been possible to detect the fake, as he had claimed.

'Nice,' Seymour said. 'Nice. I like it. This laddie could have an interesting future.'

'At the moment, he is the subject of a manhunt.'

'Oh dear,' Seymour said. 'It was him who dunnit?'

Gently shrugged.

'What a shame,' Seymour said. 'It might have been amusing to have him around. Does Sir Charles know?'

'Not yet.'

'I think I'd break the news about the picture to him first.'

'Where shall I find him?'

'Search me. But here's someone who can probably tell you.'

Brewster had come to the swing-doors, where he stood staring at the two propped-up pictures. As Gently emerged, Brewster exclaimed:

'So you've found it, then! I say ... it wasn't old Leslie, was it?'

Gently said: 'I wish to speak to Sir Charles.'

'Yes, of course. They're in the lounge. But ... ?'

Emma Spinks, too, came panting towards him. But Gently ignored both of them.

It was silent in the lounge when he entered it. Sir Charles was seated in the chair beneath the Morland painting. Next to him sat his daughter, Cassandra; at a little distance, by a tea-tray, Lady Daphne. Cups had been poured and dispensed, but a dish of cakes remained untouched. Cassandra Merton had been crying; her mother looked stern. Sir Charles met Gently with solemn brown eyes. When the door had been closed, he said:

'Any news?'

Gently nodded, and took a seat.

'Then what, man? Spit it out!'

Gently said: 'Your picture has been found.'

'Found!' Sir Charles and his lady exchanged glances. 'But where, man? Where?'

Gently said: 'On the houseboat. Secreted beneath the well floor-boards.'

175

'On the houseboat . . .'

'It appears undamaged. Superintendent Seymour is examining it now.'

'On the houseboat!'

Cassandra Merton cried: 'I knew it, I knew it, I knew it! It had to be Timothy. I said so all along. Who else could possibly have copied the painting?'

'Hush, girl, hush!' Sir Charles admonished her. 'I'm afraid I need a moment to take this in. Was Timothy there when you found the painting – have you spoken to him about it?'

Gently said: 'I advised your son that I was about to make a search. He appeared unwilling for it to proceed, and departed before the search was completed.'

'He knew it was there?'

'It would seem so.'

'But he made no admission?'

Gently shook his head.

'Then is it not possible . . . ?'

'Oh, Daddy, Daddy!' Cassandra Merton exclaimed. 'He did it, he can't not have done it. And if he did that, if . . . if . . . !'

'Quiet, girl!' Lady Daphne rapped. 'We're talking about your own brother.'

'But can't you see . . . ?'

'Stop behaving like a goose. Leave your father to sort this out.'

Sir Charles said: 'Where is Timothy now?'

Gently said: 'His precise whereabouts are uncertain.'

'Do you mean he's – cleared off?'

'He was last seen by your secretary. She saw him heading towards the forest.'

'To the forest! Then he knows you're after him?'

'I believe he understands his position.'

'And – that is?'

'We wish him to explain his possession of the picture. And, more fully, his movements on Sunday.'

Cassandra Merton stared with horrified eyes, Sir Charles with a stony gaze. But it was Lady Daphne who gave voice, after drawing herself up to glare at Gently. She said:

'Rot.'

'I beg your pardon?'

'Rot,' Lady Daphne said. 'You may think you can hang the picture on Timothy, but that's it. He didn't pot Laurence.'

'Hush, my dear!' Sir Charles said.

'Oh no,' Lady Daphne said. 'Oh no. We're talking about my son too, Charles, and I'm jolly well going to speak my mind.'

'But the facts – '

'Damn the facts. This is one of the facts too. His mother says he didn't do it, and that's the only fact that matters.'

'But, Mummy, I saw him – !' Cassandra Merton cried.

'Shut up,' Lady Daphne snapped. 'Little liar.'

'But I did – '

'You saw nobody. Or if you did, it was your precious Hugh.'

'No!'

'Just shut up – or your mother will catch you one yet.'

'Oh, Daphne, Daphne,' Sir Charles said. 'It's no use, can't you see? The one thing leads to the other. In my own mind I'm convinced that Laurence suspected what Timothy was up to.'

'I don't care, Charles.'

'At least, there are things that Timothy will have to explain.'

'I don't see why. We've found the picture. The picture never left the premises.'

'But the substitution – '

'That was a joke! He wanted to see how soon we would

177

notice it. And it was a damned fine copy, it fooled both of us, we ought to be proud of a son like that.'

'It's no use, Daphne, no use. If it was a joke, why has he run off?'

'Because – because! With all these coppers, he's scared, and daren't own up.'

Sir Charles looked at her long; then shook his head.

'Charles, I demand that you stand by him!'

'I have to look at the facts, Daphne.'

'Bugger the facts! He's our son.'

There was a timid knock at the door; after a pause, Sir Charles rapped: 'Enter!' The door opened to reveal the boiler-suited figure of the Lodge's outside-man. He said:

'I'm sorry to butt in like this, sir, but I thought you ought to know. I had to fetch something from the tack-room just now, and I found the cupboard doors ajar.'

'The doors to the gun-room?'

'Yes, sir. So I took a look in there while I was about it. And there was a gun missing, sir. And likely a box of ammo gone with it.'

'Did you notice which gun?'

'Mr Merton's spare, sir. But they tell me he's still up in the town.'

'Oh no, no!' Lady Daphne gasped. 'Timothy – oh no!'

'Thank you, Stringer,' Sir Charles said. 'You did quite right to report it.'

'Charles – we've got to stop him. We must!'

'Calm down, my dear. Calm down.'

They were on their feet now, Lady Daphne clutching at her husband's arm. Wide-eyed, Cassandra Merton had drawn near them; Gently, for the moment, was forgotten. Sir Charles rescued his arm from his wife's clutch and tenderly patted her shoulder.

'We don't know.'

'Yes. Timothy. It has to be him.'

'But even so . . .'

'He'll do it. He'll shoot himself. I know.'

'Oh, Mummy, no!' Cassandra Merton wailed.

'Yes. He'll do it. Or why else would he take a gun?'

'Hush,' Sir Charles said. 'Hush.'

'Charles, we've got to stop him. We've got to!'

Sir Charles turned anguished eyes on Gently. He said: 'You'll have men out? You're looking for him?'

Gently nodded. 'We have men in the forest. And cars patrolling the boundary roads.'

'Then there's the brecks.'

'We have summoned more men.'

'But they could be too late, man – too late!'

Gently said: 'If your son means to shoot himself, then the appearance of policemen may provoke him to it.'

'Then what – what?'

Gently said: 'An approach will be best made by a person he knows.'

'Yes – but if we don't know where he is?'

Gently stared at him: at Lady Daphne. He said: 'Your son must be familiar with the forest. He will have known it since he was a child. He may have his favourite places and, in trouble, he may make for them.'

'Gosh, yes!' Cassandra Merton exclaimed. 'Swallowdale – don't you remember? Swallows and Amazons and all that. Where we played when we were kids.'

'Swallowdale . . . ?'

'He could hide there! It's a secret place, under a big holly. If the police were hunting me, that's the place I'd jolly well head for.'

Sir Charles looked at his wife. 'What do you think?'

She shook her head. 'But we must do something!'

'If he should be there, and one of us . . . '

'He's there, I'm sure he's there!' Cassandra Merton cried.

Sir Charles turned to Gently. 'With your consent, then,

we will go to this place. Perhaps you will ensure that your men hold back and enable us to talk to him.'

Gently nodded.

'And you, yourself?'

'I shall be obliged to accompany you.'

'Oh, come on, come on!' Cassandra Merton cried. 'Nobody knows what's happening out there.'

But outside Gently made them wait while he passed the word to Calthorpe. The local man, still manning his radio, looked serious when he heard of the latest development.

'I'd best call in a couple of marksmen, sir. That gun may not be intended only for himself.'

'Just warn them to keep out of sight. And tell the men who are in there to freeze.'

'You can count on that, sir. We don't want to start another Hungerford.'

Gently left him with the radio and signalled the others to proceed. Cassandra Merton was for dashing ahead, and had to be brought to heel by Sir Charles. Gently himself stayed twenty paces in the rear. Lady Daphne was clinging to her husband's arm. Sir Charles, after a glance back at Gently, stalked grimly in the wake of his impatient daughter.

They arrived at the forest gate; Cassandra Merton led them into the main ride. If there were men in the forest, they were invisible, and the only sounds those of disturbed pigeons. Within two hundred yards a ride departed to the right, and into this Cassandra Merton directed them. Here, the going was rougher, and progress necessarily in single file. The ride rose, fell again, began to approach the open brecks. Finally, ahead, the pines gave way to what was apparently original woodland: a grove of oaks, ancient and twisted, infilled with holly that was probably as old. Cassandra Merton came to a stand and waited till Gently had joined them. Gently said:

'There?'

'Shsh! It's just round the next bend.'

'What are we looking for?'

'You won't see anything. There's a pit under one of those big hollies. It will have to be me who talks to him, because I'm the only one who knows where it is.'

Sir Charles whispered: 'It had better be me.'

'Daddy, no! I'd have to show you where. Then, if we scared him, he might clear off, because there's a back way out to the brecks.'

'The foolish boy might shoot you before he understood.'

'Just trust me, Daddy. I know Timothy.'

Then she was darting away down the track, clearly with no intention of concealment. Cautiously, Gently led the others forward, till they could just see round the shoulder of a holly. The track led into a little glade, hemmed with bushes and the tangling oaks. In the centre of the glade, before a massive holly, Cassandra Merton came to a dancing halt.

'Swallows and Amazons for ever!'

She threw her arms in the air in a girlish gesture. Did something stir in the depths of that bush? From somewhere, close, Gently heard furtive movement.

'Timmy, you ass – Timmy! I know you're in there, you raving galoot. It's no good you playing possum. It's time to come out and hold a palaver.'

Another movement? Sir Charles whispered:

'I don't think Timothy is in there at all!'

'Somewhere to the left . . .'

'Yes – and I can't forget that he's got a gun.'

Cassandra Merton danced up and down. 'Timmy!' she chanted. 'Timmy! Shiver a couple of hundred timbers – show yourself, you duffer!'

And now, wasn't the movement coming from the bush?

'Idiot brother!' Cassandra Merton sang. 'We shan't eat you. We're not cannibals. Come out, come out, wherever you are!'

181

And Timothy Stanton came out. Crawling low, like some wild beast, he emerged from under the dense swags of the holly. He got to his feet. He didn't have the gun. He stood staring wildly at those up the track. When Cassandra Merton made a move to come closer to him, he held up his hand, and started back.

'That's close enough!'

'Timmy, you chump – !'

'Stay away from me – all of you!'

'It's no use, Timmy!'

'Stay back. I didn't shoot Laurence, and I won't take the rap for it!'

'You didn't?'

'No!'

'Then who – ?'

'Who? Do I have to tell you?'

He didn't get the chance, because a gun exploded, and Timothy Stanton pitched forward on his face.

'Down – get down!'

Almost in a reflex, Gently had flattened the screaming Lady Daphne: her husband needed no telling, and Cassandra Merton had also hit the ground. The precaution was not superfluous: again the gun blasted from the hollies, shot whistled over their heads and a twig and scatter of leaves descended. Then they heard the crashing of retreating footsteps as the gunman made good his escape towards the brecks. Sir Charles scrambled up.

'The bastard! Come on, George – we can catch him!'

'No – leave him to us.'

'But he's emptied both barrels!'

'Let him go.'

'But – before he reloads!'

Gently grabbed his arm. 'First, it's your son who needs your attention.'

'Oh, Timothy – Timothy!' Lady Daphne cried; but Cassandra Merton was already at his side. In fact, he was sitting up, and shakily nursing a bloody arm. Lady Daphne threw herself down beside him. 'Timothy – Timothy! What have they done?' Tremblingly, Timothy Stanton exhibited his arm, gashed, scarred and dripping.

'Winged him,' Sir Charles said. 'He'll live. Use his shirt to bind him up.'

'Charles, you're heartless!' Lady Daphne cried.

'Never mind that. Tie him up.'

With her daughter's aid, Lady Daphne ripped the soiled sweat-shirt off her son and, with admirable dexterity, wrapped a tight bandage round the injured arm. Timothy Stanton submitted wincingly, the shock still in his distant eyes. He blurted:

'He meant it, you know. He was going to kill me. Just like Laurence.'

'Who?' Sir Charles said. 'Who was that swine?'

Timothy Stanton's shocked eyes found Gently's. Slowly, Gently nodded. He said: 'Yes. It would have to be him.'

'That photograph . . . he took it on the houseboat.'

'What was it your stepbrother saw there?'

'The fake. He saw it on the easel . . . we had to expose it, to harden the varnish.'

'And then?'

'He swore he'd tell Father.' Timothy Stanton closed his eyes. 'I went up to the house and told Dennys. He said he'd fix it . . . and he did.'

'Did he tell you how he would fix it?'

'Oh God, no! When he came back he said there'd been an accident, but it would be all right if I kept my mouth shut.'

'Did he threaten you?'

'I suppose so. He said in a showdown you'd be bound to pick me. But then the police got on to Hugh, and Dennys thought it would be safe to carry on.'

'To make the switch.'

'Yes. He'd got the buyer lined up. A Yank. It was all arranged when he was down here in the spring. He came to give an estimate on the job for Father.'

'My God, my God!' Sir Charles exclaimed. 'This can't be true. I can't believe it. And all this went on right under my eyes?'

Timothy Stanton shuddered and turned away his face.

'And meanwhile, meanwhile,' Sir Charles stormed, 'there's a killer loose on my estate – a man with a gun and plenty of ammo – who has killed one of my sons, and had a shot at the other!' He swung on Gently. 'Get him, George, if it's the last thing you do. If I had a gun I'd go after him myself. And I doubt if I'd be taking any prisoners.'

'Charles, you're mad!' Lady Daphne cried. 'We've got to get Timothy back to the house.'

'Daddy, I think he's going to faint!' Cassandra Merton cried.

And Timothy Stanton did just that.

A panting Bodney came pounding down the track, followed by one of the DCs.

'Sir, we heard shooting over here – I've called in for reinforcements!'

'We shall need a stretcher.'

'Yes, sir.'

'And the two marksmen.'

'They're on their way.'

'Let me have your set.'

Bodney handed it over. Gently switched on, and got through to control. He requested men to cover the line of the forest, and a team with dog-handlers to comb the brecks. Cars meanwhile would patrol the roads and turn back civilian traffic. 'And one more thing – ' Gently's eye was on the tearful face of Cassandra Merton. 'Get in touch

184

with Breckford, and tell them we've no more use for Hugh Merton.'

'So who is it we're after, sir?' Bodney panted.

Gently told him. 'And he has the gun.'

'And it was him who shot – ?'

'Yes. And we don't want him shooting anyone else.'

Calthorpe was the next to arrive, with two St John's Ambulance men close behind him. One of them knelt beside Timothy Stanton, while the other unstrapped a stretcher. They lifted him on to it, and prepared to leave. Sir Charles said to Gently:

'If there's anything I can do . . . '

Gently shook his head. Sir Charles hesitated for a moment, then turned away to follow the stretcher. Calthorpe said:

'Did you get a sight of him, sir?'

'He fired from cover,' Gently said.

'Like he did with the Aussie.'

'Yes.'

Calthorpe said thoughtfully: 'Getting to be a habit, sir.'

Then the dogs arrived, and the marksmen, and a body of uniformed men: Gently gave them their instructions, and the men moved off into the brecks. The dogs searched the oak thicket and the hollies, but found only the two expended shells. Crushed bracken showed where Brewster had jumped the rabbit-wire; then the trail vanished into the rough. To the right? To the left? Straight ahead? The sniffing dogs didn't have a clue. Islands of gorse, bramble, and stands of bracken provided perfect cover for the fugitive.

'Spread the dogs out.'

Tracks of a sort wove across the undulating spread of the brecks, tracks probably made by deer, but more inviting than the untrodden rough. The dog-handlers moved out left and right. Gently held a course straight ahead. With him went Calthorpe, Bodney and the marksmen, while the line of uniformed men stretched on either hand.

185

Sometimes they were visible, sometimes lost behind thick cover. At times, the group with Gently could have been alone on the sweltering brecks.

Half a mile in, Calthorpe muttered: 'Do you reckon he could have got this far, sir?'

'He had a good start.'

'He could have doubled back, sir.'

'Then he'll run into the patrols covering the forest.'

Calthorpe wiped sweat. His expression suggested that he wouldn't have disapproved of such an outcome.

The half-mile became a mile, and the blazing sun that much hotter. The dogs, at first so eager, now began to pant and to slacken stride. Then, far away to the right, came a shout, followed by another, and a third; then, bright and clear, the echoing crack of a gun. To the right: where, on its knoll, the rusting tank stood against the sky, and from it a smear of grey smoke arose, preceding a second crack of the gun.

'Move up, but stay in cover – and keep those dogs well to the rear!'

Suddenly the brecks were alive with men, as the lines of searchers began to converge.

'Spread out, some of you, and get behind him – we want that tank surrounded. But keep in cover! We're dealing with a man who doesn't hesitate to kill.'

Had he killed already? There was shouting and a scurrying amongst the gorses in the vicinity of the tank, then one saw a prone uniformed man with another kneeling beside him. And the gun cracked again: it was protruding from a port in the roofless turret of the tank.

'Stay well down!'

Another crack: and this time shot whistled close overhead. Gently dodged low round the final obstacles to reach the officer who had fallen.

'Are you badly hurt?'

'Just a scratch, sir. The bastard opened up without warning.'

His shirt, ripped open, showed a bloody chest. His companion was stripping off a field-dressing.

'It'll be all right, sir. But watch your head!'

More shot whistled into the gorses. Calthorpe, Bodney and one of the marksmen came diving in beside Gently. The marksman panted:

'Do you want me to pick him off, sir?'

'Could you?'

'I think I might just get him!'

'Or he might get you.'

'I'm ready to have a go, sir. If someone could just attract his attention.'

'Too risky.'

'The trouble is, sir, he isn't leaving much to aim at.'

'Stay in cover. At this rate, he'll soon be running short of ammunition.'

Everywhere, amongst the gorses, uniformed men were crawling into positions. Some were going wide to outflank the tank, others warily seeking points of observation. And still, at close intervals, the lead was flying, causing raised heads to be hastily ducked. Then there was a pause, though one could hear, distinctly, the click of the gun being closed after reloading.

'I'll try talking to him.'

'Better watch it, sir!'

'At a guess, he's down to his last two shells.'

'One would be enough, sir.'

'The rest of you stay back and keep your cover.'

Just ahead, and nearest to the tank, was a gorse a little isolated from its neighbours; to this gorse Gently crawled, keeping always cover between the tank and himself. He reached it. He paused. From the tank he had heard the tiniest sound: as though he had seen it, he knew the muzzle of the gun was now pointing in his direction. Keeping tight to the ground, he called:

'Dennys Brewster! Can you hear me?'

Silence answered him. He called:

'Brewster, you're wasting our time and yours. You know you can't keep this up for much longer, so why not give in now? Just throw that gun out where I can see it. We don't intend you any harm.'

Silence still.

'Brewster?'

Again silence.

'Brewster – can you hear me?'

And suddenly the bush seemed to explode over his head, accompanied by the close-at-hand crash of the gun.

'Oh, you bastard!' he heard Bodney shout; and then the gun crashed again. But this time it sounded muffled, and somehow contained in the hollowness of the tank. Gently scrambled up. Bodney came running. Uniformed men ran out of the bushes. The gun was no longer pointing through the port in the turret: and a red liquid was leaking through a drain-hole below.

'Get up and have a look.'

Bodney got up. He got down again, and was sick. He said:

'It's a good job we know who the bugger is. He must have stuck that frigging gun in his mouth.'

Gently checked. Brewster had. And oddly, the barrel of the gun had blown, too.

13

'I heard more shooting. You had better tell me the worst.'

Gently had left Calthorpe to handle matters on the brecks. The Lodge, when he arrived back there, appeared vacant and silent, but he found Phipps with Seymour in the gallery. Now apparently the best of friends again, they were occupied in replacing the (genuine) Constable in its frame. The author met Gently with a scathing stare: Seymour gave him a broad wink.

'Back from the wars, I see!' he said. 'You homicide men really live.'

'Where did they take Timothy Stanton?'

'They carted him off to the infirmary in Abbotsham.'

'Did Sir Charles go with him?'

'Just his ma and sis. I believe Sir Charles is on the phone in the study.'

Sir Charles was hanging up as Gently entered: he came forward to meet the Central Office man. In few words, Gently told him what had taken place at the old tank. Sir Charles listened in silence, his bitter gaze directed at the floor. Finally he muttered, almost to himself:

'The poor devil! I didn't wish that.'

Gently said: 'I understand your son has been taken to Abbotsham.'

Sir Charles nodded. 'I've been talking to Tommy.'

'The County Chief Constable.'

'Yes. We'd better sit down, George. Can I get you a drink?'

He went to a cabinet and poured two scotches, then they sat down on each side of the big desk. Sir Charles took a sip from his glass. He frowned at Gently, then sipped again. He said:

'All this comedy with the paintings! The fact is, the real painting never left these premises. It was never out of my son's possession. Nothing to prove positively what he meant to do with it.'

Gently said nothing. Sir Charles drank.

'It could have been a twisted joke,' he said. 'That would be well within Timothy's character, George. You've talked to him. You know what he's like.'

Gently said nothing.

'Yes, well,' Sir Charles said. 'I've been putting the point to Tommy. And he rather agrees. He says if I won't prosecute, he doesn't see any good reason why the police should. I mean, the picture's back in the gallery, and Master Timothy has had a lesson. It's all been tragic enough, Tommy thinks. And now the main culprit has met his ghastly deserts.'

Gently drank. Sir Charles drank.

'Wouldn't that be your view of it?' Sir Charles said.

Gently said: 'The prosecution to be mounted will be in the hands of the local police.'

'So – we can let it go at that?'

Gently drank. He said: 'It may be I shall offer them that advice.'

'To drop the prosecution against Timothy?'

'In the matter of the substituted painting.'

Sir Charles's eyes were like gimlets. 'But?'

'There is a more serious charge to consider.'

'I see.'

Gently said: 'Your son is innocent of the shooting of his

190

stepbrother. But he is guilty of concealing his knowledge of the culprit, and of seeking to involve an innocent man.'

'But damn it all, man! Put yourself in his position.'

'In my view, that must be left to a jury.'

'He would have come out with it, given time.'

'Again, that cannot be for me to decide.' Gently drank. He said: 'A good defence may find many things in your son's favour. It may be that, in its wisdom, the court will elect for a suspended sentence. But my advice must be to charge Timothy. He must face the consequence of what he has done. If Timothy had not been open to corruption, both your sons would be alive today.'

Sir Charles looked away. He said: 'You know how to hit where it hurts.' He finished his scotch. He said: 'Very well – perhaps it did need you to teach me my duty! And you may be right. Facing up may be the medicine Timothy needs. But I shall do my best. I shall engage the foremost defence counsel in the land. And when it's over, then we'll see. I must do something for that foolish boy.'

A vehicle crunched on the gravel of the sweep, and voices sounded on the steps, in the hall. Sir Charles was instantly on the alert. After a pause, he said:

'They're back!'

He looked at Gently: slowly, Gently shook his head.

'Damn it, you're human after all, man!' Sir Charles exclaimed; then he hastened out into the hall to meet his wife and daughter: and his pale, but walking-wounded, son.

In the gallery the Constable was rehung, and Gently found Seymour wistfully regarding the fake. Sighing, he said:

'Oh boy! If I could only borrow it to work off on the American.'

'Would it fool him?'

'Of course it wouldn't. But how I should love to try it on.'

Another car arriving on the sweep brought Calthorpe; and Gently went out to head the local man off.

Timothy Stanton was tried in the autumn by a court that did, indeed, show its wisdom. He was pronounced guilty after the fact and awarded a two-year sentence, suspended.

The following Easter, Gabrielle returned from one of her business trips to France and, after the usual preliminary exchanges, said to Gently:

'What was the name of that young painter, the one who you told me forged the Constable?'

'Why do you ask?'

'Because, my dear, I think I have met this man. As you know, I spend two days in Paris, and one morning I am visiting Montmartre. So, I happen on this pavement artist, painting such pictures as you have described to me. English, he must be. I ask him his name. He tells me it is Timothy Stanton.'

'That's the one.'

'Ha. Well, I cannot say much for this painter's talent.'

'You wouldn't rate him as a genius.'

'I think not. He is a remittance-man, do you not call it?'

'Very probably.'

'And so he will stay. That, I regret, is my opinion.'

Gently said: 'One thing is certain – a Timothy Stanton isn't a Constable!'

Gabrielle said: 'And yet, I felt sorry for him.'

Then they talked of other things.

Brundall, 1991

192